TRACES

J. T. GODDARD

Copyright © 2021 by J T Goddard

All rights reserved.

No part of this book may be reproduced in any form or by any electronic or mechanical means, including information storage and retrieval systems, without written permission from the author, except for the use of brief quotations in a book review.

The characters and events in this book are fictitious. Any similarity to real persons, living or dead, is coincidental and not intended by the author.

To Sally, Nichola, Victoria, and Kate

CHAPTER 1

I SAW THE HELICOPTERS FIRST. Three small black dots down the valley.

The afternoon sun was behind them, making them shimmer through the haze. As they got nearer, the three shook themselves apart and became five. As they passed low in front of the old ski jump towers, they became seven. By now I could see the predatory shape, recognizing them from movies and TV newscasts, and from some long-ago personal experience. Blackhawks. Attack helicopters.

They were about two kilometers away, following the highway in from the mountains. Something—intuition, experience, luck—made me slump down in front of a scrub willow. There's not much cover on Nose Hill, the largest urban park in Canada.

There are a few clumps of trees, where white tail deer lounge in the shade. There are gullies and dry creek beds, eroded by spring rain but in late summer colonized by dry brown grass. Some burrows made by rabbits, one enlarged into a den by coyotes. The meadow blazing stars had just raised their purple spikes, the spring flowers long since finished. This was August. The dog days. A hot dry summer afternoon drifting into a hot dry evening. All quiet on the western horizon. Except for seven attack helicopters.

I could now hear the chattering thump thump thump of the rotors. They were moving right to left across my line of vision, heading towards the city. Then the pitch of the engines changed. The formation broke apart.

Two kept going straight, towards the city centre. Two rose and peeled left, passing to my side and over the ridge behind me. Two peeled right, following the highway down across the river and to the south of the city. One seemed to pause, just holding its position between me and the university campus. Then the rockets came.

I couldn't believe what I was seeing. In front of me, less that a kilometer away, the tower of the university library suddenly exploded. The walls appeared to lift upwards for a split second, then the whole edifice collapsed. To the east of my viewpoint, the revolving restaurant symbolic of the city simply disintegrated, leaving the pinnacle of the tower. The glass frontage of City Hall took a direct hit, as did many of the office towers that housed the oil companies and financial giants of the western economy. In the far distance, columns of smoke rose from the southern reaches of the city. Critical infrastructure, I supposed. Bridges, interchanges, tunnels for the suburban train lines. That's what I would have done.

Behind me I heard explosions. The airport, I guessed, and perhaps the refinery that lay just north of the city. The helicopter in front of me turned a lazy arc, away from the university, and then casually strafed the cars and trucks still streaming down the highway. I hunched deeper into my willow.

When the firing stopped, I expected silence. But the noise was still there, even louder now, and discordant in its lack of purpose. Car horns and vehicle alarms wailed, explosions continued to reverberate, the whump whump of the helicopters grew louder. I realized that they were regrouping, coming together over the river. They circled twice until all seven were present, then turned in a line and flew west.

I watched them pass in front of me again, this time left to right. The sun had dipped down towards the mountains. It must have been almost directly in the eyes of the pilots. The land below was the crackling brown of a western summer. The sky above was an intense but washed out white. Only the mountains held their form.

The helicopters diminished in size, then appeared to merge momentarily with a larger blur. That blur continued to advance through the haze. As it came towards the old ski jumps it too took shape. Large black planes, each with two engines. The signature pot belly fuselage of the Globemaster was missing, so I guess these were Hercs. Three of them.

Like the helicopters before them, the group peeled apart in front of me. One came back and across to my left, towards the airport. The second maintained its heading, over the city centre. The third cut south, towards what used to be the Canadian Forces Base. This was now decommissioned, but I knew that in addition to the upscale housing and trendy farmers' market that had replaced the parade squares, it still housed the headquarters of the 41 Canadian Brigade Group. I could guess what would happen next.

Sure enough, from the back of each plane a series of black dots appeared, falling away before the parachutes opened. From where I sat, the setting sun which was slowly reddening the landscape also highlighted the white silk. It was strangely beautiful. The targets seemed to be the airport, the city centre, and the army headquarters. The paratroopers descended into the smoke and chaos of a city in turmoil. It must have been one of the quickest and easiest occupations in history.

The sun disappeared, leaving an afterglow to backlight the mountains. I stood up carefully, used my boot to scuff some loose dirt back into the coyote den. In the dusk I picked my way down from the hill.

I had been out for an afternoon walk so my clothes were dry and comfortable, but they wouldn't do for a prairie night. I could already feel a chill. Once on the streets I kept to the back alleys. I could hear people outside their doors, talking over the fences, asking each other what was going on.

By the time I got to the house I had heard that there had been similar attacks in Vancouver, Edmonton, Saskatoon, Regina, Brandon, and Winnipeg. All of western Canada, it seemed, had been invaded. I slipped inside and bolted the door behind me. I left the lights off, as I tried to figure out what to do next.

First, I called my wife. Estranged wife. Such an unusual word, estranged. Lots of definitions. In our case, it meant "I don't like the west, I don't like Calgary." The dryness of the air. The electric crackle of the thunderstorms. The crowds in the streets. The casual racism. The ongoing quest for money. The pseudo cowboy culture. Men in big black Stetsons and women in stilettos. Everyone from somewhere else, and wanting to go somewhere else, to retire to the mountains or the coast. The neoconservative religious ethic held by men who frequented casinos and strip clubs. The huge trucks. The permanent rush hour. The macho disregard for anyone other than self. But I had a job.

She took the girls to visit her parents. Northern Ontario. Pine trees and cold clear lakes. Small town bonhomie. Proper winters, where the snow came and sat for three months. No chinooks. No icy wide streets with the winds howling. Solid brick houses with their own front and back gardens. Friends from an earlier life. The girls like it here, I've enrolled them in day camps. We might stay a bit longer. You have a job.

It took three tries before I got through. The cell system was down, so I used the landline. Are you OK? What on earth is happening?

Nothing here, it's quiet in the Soo. The news says that the Americans are fed up with having to import coal and lumber. They need fresh water, and we won't let them buy any. The natural resources are wasted in the north, nobody lives there. We're shipping oil to China and the eastern provinces, they need it in California. So, they've decided to come and take it.

What, the oil?

Everything.

There's a road block at Falcon Lake, the highway between Ontario and Manitoba has been cut. The news shows lots of soldiers, theirs and ours. Tanks. Barbed wire. Airspace has been closed over Ontario. Planes are being rerouted, to Montreal, Halifax, Gander. What are you going to do?

I don't want to be an American. I don't want to be occupied. My job was at the university and I've just seen it bombed. I miss my girls. I miss you. I'm going to get to the Soo. I'll see you soon.

They've closed the border. There are no planes. The roads are blockaded. The trains are cancelled. What are you going to do, walk?

Yes.

It was a pretty easy decision, really. And once it was made, it set, like a new concrete sidewalk. It might take some time but it was better than sitting in this dark suburban house, waiting for a knock at the door.

It's miles. Hundreds, no thousands, of miles. Three thousand. Kilometers. Remember it took us three days of driving. No, four days. Calgary to Regina. Regina to Winnipeg. Winnipeg to Thunder Bay. Thunder Bay to the Soo. Four days of driving. Ten hours a day.

But that was in the car, with the kids. The actual driving was less than that.

The distance was the same, though. And we made about a hundred klicks an hour. Clear roads. No army patrols. No helicopters shooting up the traffic. It's not like that now.

I know. And I won't be walking down the highway. Listen, I have to go.

But

No. I can't stay here. I'm going to leave my phone, someone could track me. So you won't hear from me for a while. Maybe a few months. But I'm coming, to see you, to see my girls.

It's crazy.

Listen, I saw it happen. I was in the park, up on Nose Hill. I saw them bombing the Tower. I saw them strafing the cars on Crowchild. I saw the paratroopers. It's crazy to stay here.

But how

Remember the traders? Remember Samuel Hearne and

David Thompson? Peter Pond? They came here from Montreal, for god's sake. They had no cars, no phones. They didn't even know where they were going. I have maps, I can figure out a route. I have better clothes than they did. Better dried food. I think maybe three, four months. I'll be there for Christmas.

No you won't. I'll never see you again.

You'll never see me again if I stay here.

But

Set a place for me at Christmas dinner.

But

Look, I've got to go. Give the girls each a big kiss from me. Love you.

Love you too, but

No buts. See you at Christmas.

But

I have to go. Like I said, I'm leaving my cell phone here but I'll get in touch when I can.

Christmas?

Yes.

Promise?

Yes.

I hang up and take a deep breath, then go down to the basement. All the hiking and camping gear is there. I take out the things I think I'll need, pack a rucksack. It weighs about a hundred and twenty pounds. I doubt if I can carry it to the end of the street. I unpack it and start again.

In the end I have a small backpack. Two changes of clothes, one to wear and one to wash. Two pairs of walking boots, one to wear now and one for when those wear out. A good hunting knife. Fork, Spoon. Cup. Dish. Water purification tablets. Matches, lots of matches, which I put in little zip-lock bags. My small hand axe. A lightweight sleeping bag and tarpaulin. Some fishing line, a dozen hooks and lures. A couple of maps showing the main river systems of the prairie provinces, including the north. A camping saucepan and frying pan combination. I know that I have probably forgotten something.

I leave my phone, my camera. I take a small notebook, a few pens. It would be good to keep some sort of diary. It's a long way. I add a second notebook. Another pen. A compass would help. I search around and find it, eventually, in the bag with the tent pegs. I leave the tent. I go through my wallet and take out all the loyalty cards. I keep my health card, driver's licence, social insurance card. My bankcard. I leave the rest, then put my credit card back in, just in case. I think I'm ready. I take my backpack and go upstairs.

Will I have enough food? There is nothing in the fridge, some wilted lettuce and two slices of cold pizza. There is stuff in the big white chest freezer but I can't take that. In the cupboards I find some sachets of dried food, past their sell-by date but hopefully still edible. I put them in the pack.

It's nearly dark and the streetlights have come on. The house lights are still off. I hear an engine and see an armoured car slowly drive past, a searchlight seeking out the dark corners alongside houses and behind hedges. I duck down behind the couch, even though I know they can't see me. I'm trembling.

The noise of the engine dies away. I see the glint of a reflected streetlight from a bottle of Ardbeg on the side table. I pour a small one and sip it, slowly. Think back to the movies I've seen. Gloves. And some black shoe polish. I won't put that on now, though. It goes in my backpack. A baseball cap, and some bug spray. I find three half-used cans and stuff them in. What else? Toilet paper. I have room for two rolls, after that it will be leaves.

I sip my scotch, the smoky taste lingering. Should I take some? No, I'll need a clear head. And a plan. Getting out of the city will be the hardest part. I go back to the basement and look at my map of Calgary. I'm in the northwest. The main roads will be blocked. I use my finger to trace out a route. Before I turn off the light, I remember something else. A flashlight. And a couple of extra batteries. I turn off the switch and go back upstairs.

My backpack feels heavy but not too bad. I pull on a black fleece. Find a dark toque, a scarf. Shoulder the backpack and check that all the doors are locked. Go out through the connecting door to the garage. Lock it behind me. That's it, I'm committed now. My keys are on the small table next to my chair. Next to my unfinished scotch. I open the small back door of the garage and peer out into the garden. Nobody there. The streetlight in front of the house doesn't reach here. The one in the alley is burned out.

Back in the garage I turn on the low wattage bulb and look at the electric bike. It is an old model but charged up. I take off the headlight and taillight cover and remove the bulbs. There is an identification disc attached to the frame. I bang it with a hammer, trying to snap it off, but it is welded on and simply bends. It will be harder to read now, at least.

I turn off the overhead light. Open the back door again and gently ease the bike out into the garden. Close the door behind me. Walk to the back fence, open the gate. Nobody around. I climb on the bike, adjust my backpack so it's sitting comfortably. Start to pedal. The engine kicks in, and I glide rapidly to the first cross alley. Down it to the next. And the next.

Money. That's what I need. There's an ATM in the convenience store next to the coffee shop. I sit on the bike and watch for a few minutes, then ride down the alley and park next to garbage bins. The coffee shop is quiet. Two old guys sitting in a corner. The girl rinsing out a coffee pot, someone else moving behind her in the back kitchen. I buy a small double double and add sugar, I think I'll need the energy. Next door I pick up a chocolate bar and make two withdrawals from the ATM. There's a limit on each one, and a maximum for the day, but eight hundred bucks should see me for a few days at least.

"Who was that masked man?"

Outside the store are the two old guys from the coffee shop. I'd forgotten to take off my scarf, wrapped around my face to try and stop me swallowing dust. The old men looked at me but spoke to each other.

"What's a young man doing out on the street alone at this time of the evening?"

"They said on the news they wanted everyone under fifty to report to a police station."

"Not valligant."

"Gallivant."

"Whatever. Not be out getting money from a cash machine."

"While wearing a backpack."

"Like he was going somewhere."

"Running away?"

"Like that Cohen song. 'I slipped across the border, when the soldiers came'."

"No gun, though."

"Money to buy one."

"Yup."

They stopped talking and looked at me. One to each side of the sidewalk. A bit younger than I had thought. Not much, but enough. Late fifties or early sixties, probably. Straight backed. When I reached into my pocket they tensed and moved slightly further apart. Ex-military, I decided. If I go for one, the other will get me.

"Relax," I said, pulling out my wallet.

"Can I donate a twenty to each of you, for the Legion?"

The one on the left smiled a little.

"Nope."

"Forty?"

"Each?"

"Yup."

"Nope," said the one on the right. He didn't smile.

"A nice round number would be better."

I sighed, peeled off five twenties, handed them over. They nodded at me, then walked off into the darkness.

I went back behind the coffee shop. My bike was still there, thank god. I eased it off the stand and pedalled silently away, the motor kicking in. As I crossed the first alley two shadows peeled away from the wall. They watched me glide past. One raised his arm.

"Hi ho, Silver, away!" he called.

They melted back into the darkness, and I rode silently through the quiet streets until suddenly I was past the last row of townhouses and into open country. I stopped and looked back. There was a slight knoll, the rich houses at the top, facing out across the prairies. The rows of townhouses massed beneath them, a blank area of grass dividing the two worlds.

The houses at the top looked like a herd of muskox, standing shoulder to shoulder, gazing outward in search of danger. Beneath their feet the lemmings, crammed together, moving in a mass each morning and afternoon, now safely tucked into their burrows. I looked at my watch. It was just after eleven. There was a small sliver of a moon, and what seemed like a lot of stars. I turned back to the road, kick started the bike, and began heading north.

CHAPTER 2

I FIGURED that I would get fifty or sixty kilometres from the bike before the battery failed. That would get me nearly to Didsbury, as long as there were no problems along the way. I was on the old range road, cutting straight north. It ran between the scenic foothills route of Highway 22 and the six lane expressway between Calgary and Edmonton.

I hoped that any security would be on those roads, not on this thin line of asphalt running between huge fields of canola, cattle, and grain. Not that I could see any of that detail. The stars provided some faint light, enough to see the road, but even the fence line beyond the ditch was difficult to discern.

Now and then I saw the yard light of a farmhouse, set a few hundred feet back from the road. Twice a dog barked as I rode by, but they were disinterested barks and no households were awakened with a blaze of light. I surprised a skunk on one stretch but swerved to avoid him, and got past without being sprayed.

The only real incident came when headlights appeared in front of me. They were some way away, so I stopped the bike and jumped off, then walked it down into the ditch. The spring runoff can be heavy in central Alberta, and the ditch accumulates the excess water and leads it away down the edges of the fields. Sometimes there are culverts, where an access road leads to a field for the farmer to check the crop, or an oil company worker to service one of the nodding donkeys that scatter the countryside.

But I didn't have time to find a culvert. I stepped into the ditch, which in late summer had accumulated coffee cups, beer cans, bottles, fast food wrappers, and the other detritus of rural life. I laid the bike on the road side of the ditch, hoping that the edge would cast a shadow over it, then lay down a few metres further north.

I could hear the vehicle now, approaching quickly. A shimmer of light seemed to fill the air, and as it intensified, I tucked my face into my hands and lay as still as I could, hoping no bare skin was visible. The truck roared past, its headlights passing over both me and the bike, and then it was gone.

I lay in the ditch for another ten minutes or so, my heart racing, wondering if a passenger had happened to look out and see something, and was even now encouraging the driver to stop and turn around. But nothing happened, and after a while I sat up and looked around. Silhouetted against the stars, two horses peered at me across the top of the fence. One puffed a breath of air, as if to ask me why I was lying in a ditch, while the other simply shook its ears and walked away.

I walked back to my bike and picked it up. It didn't seem damaged from having been thrown to the ground. I hunched over and pressed the button on the side of my watch, hiding the illuminated screen. It was just after one in the morning. I got back on the bike and started peddling. The battery clicked on, and I continued north.

It was an hour or so later that I saw a soft glow on the horizon. At first I thought it was the dawn, but it was too early for that, and lay to the north not the east. The light grew steadily bigger as I pedalled towards it, and soon I identified it as the small town of Didsbury. Once I got there I would have travelled about sixty kilometers, and it would be time to turn east. However, I had no idea of the situation in Didsbury, or anywhere else for that matter, so I didn't want to simply go cruising into the town.

I slowed down even more from my steady fifteen kilometers an hour, although by now my knees hoped I would slow down to a stop. I continued along, paying more attention to my surroundings. I was looking for something specific and it wasn't long until I found it. The bulk of an old farmhouse stood across to my right.

There were no lights on, except for a security light on a pole in the yard. There were no cars or trucks in the driveway that I could see, no farm machinery parked up against the barn. As I approached, I saw that there was an old five bar gate, hanging between two tall poles. The gate was closed. Over my head the poles were linked by a massive beam, which probably bore the name of the ranch, etched into it with a branding iron, although I couldn't see that detail in the dark.

What I could see, though, was a small rectangular board nailed to the gate. It was white, and the writing was legible. "For Sale" it said, together with the name and telephone number of the realtor. The double strand barbed wire fence came up to the posts on each side, but I lay the bike down and pushed it under the gate. I clambered through the bars myself, pulled up the bike, and cautiously approached the house. I kept stopping to listen, but other than the sounds of my feet and the wheels on the gravelled drive, there was nothing.

Once I got into the yard, I left the bike leaning up against the side of the barn, and walked slowly around the house itself. No dog started barking, no light came on. The shadows from the security light bounced about and made me jump a couple of times, but it was obvious that the house was empty. At the back door I risked bringing out my flashlight.

The door was locked, of course, with one of those combination locks that control access to people who have the code, but down to the side I found what I was looking for, an outside socket. I went back to the barn and got my bike, then wheeled it up to the back door. The cord from the battery charger reached, and I was delighted to see the amber light start flashing. I left the battery on charge, covering the blinking light with a small piece of plywood I found lying in the grass. I had to hope that no potential purchaser came out to the farm today, there was no way I could hide the cord hanging down from the socket.

I took the bike back to the barn. The side door was clasped, not locked, and with the edge of my knife I soon had the screws undone. I carefully opened the door and edged inside. Something rustled away to my left, and from above me I heard restless cooing from what were probably pigeons. I brought the bike inside, closed the door, and turned on my flashlight.

I was cautious about the light shining through chinks in the walls, so I masked the light with my hand. That didn't work too well, so I pulled my spare shirt from the backpack and used that as a filter. The light was dimmed, but I could see enough.

The barn was basically empty. There were a couple of old tires and some tools stacked along one wall, some clumps of straw on the concrete floor at the far end, just in front of a small door, and a large plastic drum of some kind sitting over by the main door. That was it. No car waiting quietly to be stolen, no truck to blend into the Alberta landscape. Nothing.

I went back to the yard and looked around the yard again. From this angle I could see the side of the house, and I recognized the coiled shape of a hosepipe. I went over and checked and, sure enough, one end was lying on the ground and the other was attached to a tap about three feet up the wall. I turned the tap, it was stiff but opened, and a trickle came out the other end of the hose. I went back to the barn and got my cup, and a saucepan. I filled my cup first, in case the water was shut off and I was only getting the residue, then left it to flow for a few minutes.

The water splashed onto the farmyard and after three or four minutes I filled the saucepan. I rinsed out the cup, refilled it, and took a drink. It tasted OK, like water should, and I realized that I was thirsty. I drank the cup, refilled it, and turned off the tap. There was nothing to be done about the water splash, glistening softly in the early light of dawn, so I left it and took my containers back to the barn.

I kicked some straw together and covered it with my tarpaulin, then laid out the sleeping bag on top. I went back to the door and edged it a little bit open, then put a brick against the back to keep it in place. I put the saucepan of water carefully on top of the door, resting across onto the lintel. That would confuse someone who came in, I thought, and wake me up so that I was not totally surprised. I checked the small door behind me, it creaked open without difficulty. I felt more comfortable now that the main access was alarmed, after a fashion, and the secondary exit was close by. I put my knife under the poncho I had rolled up into a pillow, climbed into my sleeping bag, and fell asleep.

When I woke up it took me a minute to remember where I was. It was dark inside the barn but not black – more a dull grey, like a foggy morning on the coast. A thin sliver of light came in from the door and made a bright sharp line across the floor like an abstract painting. My watch showed me it was nearly four o'clock, I had slept for more than ten hours.

All that fresh air and fun, I supposed. My legs ached and I was hungry. I eased out of the sleeping bag and stood up, slowly trying to stretch muscles that had not been used to so much pedalling.

At the door I carefully brought down the saucepan, then eased open the frame. The light was intense after the barn, and it took my eyes some moments to adjust. There was no sound, and I couldn't see anyone or anything, so I opened the door more fully and stepped outside. A huge racket from my right caused me to stumble back in fright, then relax as five or six pigeons wheeled up and over the farmhouse. I stepped out again. The yard was empty.

I walked slowly around the house and was pleased to see that the light on the bike battery was pulsing green. In the shadow of the porch I stopped to urinate, experiencing relief as I did. I finished my circuit and got back to the barn. From my bag I took a sachet of dehydrated soup, chicken and vegetable according to the label, and my mug. Then I realized that I had not brought my camping stove.

I wasn't sure what to do. If I lit a fire, even a small one, there was a danger that someone might see the smoke and either come to check it or, worse, report it to the authorities. If I waited until dark then the smoke would not be visible, but the flicker of a fire might be, and woodsmoke has a pungent aroma that carries for miles. The electricity was still working and there would probably be a stove in the house, but surely an empty house in the country would have an alarm system connected to the local police detachment. I could not risk breaking in and triggering an alarm.

Finally, I made my decision, and emptied the soup flakes into my camping mug. I added water from the saucepan, a few drops at a time, and stirred the concoction with my spoon. Once I had it in a thick paste, I drank a gulp of water, then proceeded to eat the cold mush.

I have eaten worse. It was dry and dusty to the taste, even though it was a paste, and every so often a kernel of some unidentifiable vegetable got stuck between my teeth or caught in the back of my throat. At those times I drank some more water and told myself that my body would be grateful for the nutrients, whatever the taste.

When I had finished, I rinsed out my cup and spoon, repacked my bag, and went behind the house for the battery. I replaced it in the bike, making sure that all the connections were tight, then sat back and waited for dark.

As I SAT in the barn, I reflected on what I was doing. I knew there had been some sort of military incident, apparently an invasion, and that the city where I lived had been occupied. I had some vague idea of why, based on those overheard conversations, but no sense of the scale of things.

Was life in the rural areas continuing more or less as normal, life inconvenienced but not disrupted, or was there a jackboot of occupation stepping out across all the land? It had only been just over twenty-four hours, after all; how much could have been achieved in that time? Surely this would have been a period of consolidation, making sure that the main targets were secure. Cities and major transportation links, perhaps, but not the rural communities.

Not yet anyway. Perhaps—and hopefully—I had a small window of opportunity. If the rural areas were to be the second phase, then the north would be the third, and I had a chance to keep ahead of any security forces that might be trying to impose control.

If what the two old soldiers who had robbed me had said was true, then the biggest problem I faced was keeping out of sight. If the police were registering everyone under 50, and presumably issuing some sort of identity card, I didn't have one. That could be awkward if I was stopped. Better not be stopped, then, I thought, just keep out of sight. Travel at night, rest during the day.

As the barn slowly darkened, I reviewed my plan, such as it was. I hoped to travel north and east, zig-zagging my way along backroads until I reached the North Saskatchewan River. Then I'd travel down that venerable waterway to Lake Winnipeg, cross the lake at a narrow point, and bushwhack the last hundred kilometres or so to the border.

Well, not bushwhack exactly, more follow old logging roads and the like, but make my way east until I was in Ontario. Then south to a main road and find a ride that would take me to the Soo. That was doable in three months,

I thought. The fur traders had made that journey every fall, taking pelts from the lake country of northern Alberta and Saskatchewan back to the merchants of Montreal. If they could do it, so could I; they hadn't had electric bikes.

On that thought I smiled and checked to see if it was dark enough to travel. I could see the glow of Didsbury on the horizon, to the north, and to the west the lingering light as the sun dropped behind the mountains. I gazed at the line of peaks, standing backlit and silhouetted against the sky. I was going to be heading east and didn't know when I would see that skyline again.

An old Ian Tyson song came to mind, something about 'where the rimrock meets the sky', and it seemed a perfect description for the etched ridge. I turned my back on the mountains and looked to the darkness which lay east.

Rolling the bike out of the barn, I carefully closed the door behind me. Adjusted the backpack to make it comfortable. Took a final look around, and saw an old horseshoe lying on the dirt. I picked it up and slipped it into a side pocket of my pack. Lucky for some, I thought. I readjusted the pack, stepped onto the bike, and pedalled back to the road.

CHAPTER 3

For the first while I continued north, the lights of Didsbury getting brighter, and then I turned onto a road which cut to the east. This was more travelled than the Range Road and three times I found myself lying in the ditch hoping that a driver, or more likely a passenger, did not look down as they drove past.

I made good time, though, and it was not even midnight when I realized that the humming in my ears was the sound of traffic on a major highway. Soon afterwards I started to see the glow of headlights moving at right angles in front of me. I knew I was approaching my next big challenge—how to get across the Queen Elizabeth II Highway, the major road artery between Calgary and Edmonton.

A few hundred metres from the busy road I came to the slipway which took traffic down to the highway. Cars coming off the highway would come up opposite, I reasoned, and a quick dash across the road confirmed this. I backtracked a hundred metres and looked around. The light was poor, for there was still only a thin moon, but in the field to my right I could see large round hay bales.

They must have been freshly cut, for they still scented the air.

Over the road, to my left, a herd of cows mooed and rustled, some standing while others lay quietly along the fence. I laid the bike down in the ditch, making a half-hearted attempt to cover it with weeds, brush, and the general detritus in which it lay. Then I climbed through the fence and hunkered down next to the nearest hay bale. Realizing that I could not see anything except my small road, I dashed to the next bale, and then the next, until I had a decent view of the highway.

The road along which I had travelled now lay to my left, cutting a straight line to the overpass that carried it across the highway. The slip road curved in front of me. There was steady traffic on the highway, which surprised me. Perhaps things were not as bad as I had anticipated.

As I watched, though, I realized that this was not regular car traffic. It was mainly trucks, long convoys of them, escorted front and back by military vehicles. They were heading in both directions. Once a slower convoy laboured past, all armoured personnel carriers, the headlights of each illuminating the antenna and gun turrets on the one in front.

The traffic continued for another hour, then stopped. Suddenly there was silence: no trucks, no vehicles. It was as though a switch had been pulled. I sat by my hay bale in the dark and wondered if I could simply ride over the bridge.

My thoughts were interrupted by a bright spotlight that suddenly beamed out of the sky, shining directly on the overpass. The beam illuminated a fox, which stopped for a moment and then ran forward. The light tracked it for a few seconds and then switched off as the fox reached the end of the bridge and slipped into the paddock with the cows.

These moved around and murmured, then were quiet once more.

It seemed that there was some sort of drone, either stationary over the bridge or moving up and down the highway. It must have a motion-sensor or something that picked up body heat, because I hadn't seen the fox at all and I had been staring at the bridge. This was going to make crossing the highway more difficult.

I sat for another hour, considering, and as my eyes grew more accustomed to the dark, I was able to see the drone. It was a long pale thing, shaped like the paper aeroplanes we used to make as kids but obviously bigger. About six feet in length, I thought, but with each wing twice that size.

It passed over the bridge every fifteen minutes, first heading north before coming back south, then north again, so it must have been on a programmed circuit. No doubt it was covering three or four of the bridges which cut across this section of the highway.

No doubt there was a drone operator somewhere, in Calgary or in Colorado, who was watching a screen and waiting for body heat or movement to be registered.

Fifteen minutes. Could I scurry across the bridge in that time, I wondered. If the sensors were only at the front then I would have seven minutes, after it crossed the overpass and before it turned at the end of its route. But if there were sensors at the back as well, then I would only have a minute or two when it was at the far end of its orbit, when I might have a chance that the range was too far for it to pick me up.

That was a risky proposition and would require perfect timing and a lot of luck. I would be on my bike, which would give me the advantage of speed across the bridge, but once over I would be trapped on the road. If the drone spotted me, it would catch me quite easily. I wasn't sure I liked the odds.

I SAT A WHILE LONGER, thinking. The bike was comfortable, but I only got fifty or sixty kilometres before I had to recharge the battery. I could not count on finding a vacant farmhouse with connected power every night.

It was late August, and the days were starting later and finishing earlier. It was basically dark by nine each evening, and the first tinges of dawn did not appear much before six in the morning. So that gave me a good nine hours each night, and if I was able to walk at a regular speed then I should make five or six kilometres an hour. So, without the bike I could make about the same distance, as long as I could keep moving steadily.

The idea came to me shortly after that, about three in the morning. I went back to the bike and pulled more debris over it, covering it as thoroughly as I could. I picked up my pack, then crossed the road and found the gate which opened onto the paddock. I pulled it open, then walked in a big circle around the cows.

There were about ten of them in this group, and they muttered and shuffled to their feet as I smacked their rumps. Once moving, though, they kept going. I herded them out onto the road then turned them to the left, towards the highway. They ambled slowly, and I didn't rush them. I watched the space above the bridge and saw the drone pass, heading south. I kept herding the cattle forward and after twelve minutes dropped into the ditch.

The first two cows were just starting across as the drone returned, hovered, then shone its spotlight down. The cows kept moving, the next pair following the first onto the bridge, and the drone slowly rotated in place. I didn't move as the beam came around towards me, the edge spilling into the ditch but the main focus on the cows. The light held steady for a few moments, then switched off. I lay still, risking a slow raise of my head so that I could look forward. The drone moved forward and was gone.

I ran up out of the ditch and jinked in between the first six cows and the last four. They and I walked across the bridge together. It seemed to take an eternity, but by my watch it was only eleven minutes before the first two were on the other side. I moved, then, quickly trotting in between the cattle until I too was across the bridge and could dive into the nearest ditch. I pulled my toque down low and waited.

Another two minutes passed, and then the drone lit up the bridge once more. There were only two cows still in the process of wandering across, and the spotlight moved over the other eight which were already on the eastern side of the highway. Checking the numbers, I thought. Then the spotlight was switched off, the drone flew away to the south, and I climbed out of the ditch and ran as fast as I could down the road.

TEN MINUTES later I was once again in the ditch, this time waiting for a car to pass. I could see its headlights coming from some way distant and had found a small shrubby bush to curl up against. This vehicle seemed to be going slower than the others which I had encountered and as it passed by, I realized why. It was an old jeep, towing a box car trailer, and both had seen better days.

After it had wheezed past, I moved to the other side of the shrub, so I could watch. It kept going up the road and then stopped just before reaching the bridge. Two men climbed down, opened the back door of the trailer, and a low ramp was pulled, screeching, into place. The men rounded up the cattle with a wide variety of whoops and hollers, counting them into the trailer, then secured the ramp and door back in place.

I lay behind my shrub for another ten minutes or so while they slowly executed a seventeen-point turn, then drove back past me and returned from whence they had come. As the taillights faded from sight I got slowly to my feet, looked around, and then started walking, following the same path as the truck.

I walked for about three hours before I saw the first false dawn start to light the sky ahead of me. There had been no more traffic, so I had been able to keep a steady pace. During the first hour I had passed by a farmhouse where the yard lights were blazing, the old jeep parked in the yard. I could hear the muffled curses as the men unloaded the cattle from the trailer and shooed them into a paddock.

A dog barked, probably at me, but was ignored, no doubt because the men could not see beyond their circle of light. I kept moving steadily, and the barking soon stopped.

Later I passed other farms, some with a security light shining over the yard and others in darkness, but I did not stop to investigate. I just kept walking, trying to put as much distance as possible between me and the highway.

It was only when the horizon began to lighten that I started to look for a place to spend the day. This was grain country, it seemed, long flat fields with not much cover. Houses were few and far between. I was starting to get concerned when the road suddenly had railings on each side, the first time I had seen such a fence. I walked to the nearest one and peered over.

Beneath me was a concrete channel, some sort of aqueduct or canal, a thin trickle of green water flowing along the base. The sides and edges were poured concrete, straight lines etched across the prairie. It must be for irrigation, I thought, or else for flood control in the spring. Either way, at the end of summer it was running dry.

I walked to the end of the guard rails and then carefully made my way across the ditch, over the wire strands of the fence, and then down into the channel. Kneeling down, I peered under the bridge which roofed the culvert. There was a small semi-circle of light at the other side of the road, and various cans, branches, plastic bags, and other rubbish strewn about. But I could not see or hear any animals, or people, so I slowly crawled under the arch.

It was about four feet high at the apex, so I could sit with my back against the wall. I used my feet and hands to slowly clear myself a small space. I tried not to dislodge material into the channel, as I did not want either to dam the canal or to send a tell-tale stream of refuse floating through the fields.

Most of the cans I piled up, the plastic bags and paper wrappings beneath them, the larger branches on top. I found an old thimble, the type my grandmother had used to protect her fingers when sewing, and wondered how it had got there. I put it into my pocket, for good luck I suppose and because you never know when something might be useful.

I was feeling hungry but could not face the idea of more

uncooked dry soup. I had some water left and sipped that a little. Tomorrow I need to replenish supplies, I thought. I needed to fill my water bottles and find some food. I estimated that I was about half-way between Didsbury and the badlands near Drumheller, so that would be my goal for the next day. Once I was through the badlands I could turn left, and head north to the river. On that thought I lay down on the concrete shelf, my jacket as my pillow, and went to sleep.

CHAPTER 4

It was still light when I woke up. I lay still for a moment, trying to recall where I was, why I was lying on a concrete floor in the half-light of early evening. Slowly things came back to me, and I forced myself to sit up. The curve of the culvert hunched me forward enough that I could see clearly out from each end.

To my right, the thin sluice ran straight between fields of yellow, perhaps mustard or canola, I couldn't remember which bloomed last. The contrasts between the rigidity of the man-made line and the yellow fluttering flowers of the crop were intense. The sky had started to darken, but the flares of a prairie sunset were visible at the horizon. It would make a wonderful photograph, I thought. I turned to my left and found myself looking down the barrel of a gun.

The man holding it was kneeling on the same ledge as me, but back towards the opening. He looked older than me, with a short, trimmed beard and hair cut so it only reached to the collar of his red and black plaid shirt. Over that he wore an old oilskin jacket, frayed along the hem. His baseball cap showed that he was a football fan.

"Go Riders," I said.

He looked at me, then reached up with his left hand and took off his cap. His right hand never wavered; the gun never trembled. He looked at the front of his cap, as if to remind himself, then put it back on.

"This here's a Stampeders' cap."

"I know. But I'm a Riders fan."

"I'm holding a gun on you and you want to talk football?"

His voice had risen half an octave, this time the gun did tremble.

"Just making conversation."

"Come out here where I can see you."

He backed out slowly, still on his knees, still pointing the gun at me. I crawled out after him, dragging my jacket and backpack with me. As I reached the mouth of the culvert, he told me to wait, stood up, and looked around. Then he gestured me to stand.

We looked at each other. He was about my size, just older by about ten years. His face was tanned and lined by the sun. he wore dirty blue jeans and scuffed brown cowboy boots, with pointed toes and some sort of inscribed design. I kept my hands out by my sides, my backpack hanging from one, my jacket from the other. He kept the rifle pointed at me.

"What's in the bag?"

"Just my gear. Spare clothes. Camping stuff."

"Any weapons?"

"No."

"None at all?"

"I have a hunting knife, that's it."

"Where is it?"

"Here, on my belt."

I put my bag down and placed my jacket on top, then pulled at the hem and lifted my sweater so he could see the sheath looped onto my belt.

"Throw it here."

I started to unclasp the sheath, but he stopped me.

"No. Undo your belt. Throw the whole thing."

I did as he asked. It landed just in front of him and he caught it with his boot, pulled it to and behind him. It might have been my imagination, but he seemed to relax a little. The gun never moved, though.

"How did you find me?"

I was genuinely interested, but he only laughed.

"The dog," he said, gesturing up behind me. I looked around. Silhouetted up on top of the culvert was a sharp faced dog, head on its paws, looking straight at me. Its nose had a long white streak, I guess on a horse it would be called a blaze, for the snout was otherwise black. Its ears were pointed, its eyes were bright. It looked intelligent and alert.

"That's Badger. He's the one who barked when you came past the farm, after you pulled that stunt with the cows. I shut him up, I was too tired to deal with you last night. I figured I'd see where you went, catch you up today. And here we are."

He gave a short whistle and Badger leapt down off the road, then sat at his side. The dog was coloured like a border collie, black and white, but was low slung and had a longer body than I had expected. Its tail was short and spikey, black with a white tip, like a flag.

"He tracked me?"

"Uh-huh. We started after lunch, been here a while now, waiting for you to wake up."

We looked at each other. I tried to think of something intelligent to say.

"Thanks for letting me sleep."

"You're welcome. Plus, it meant you weren't on the road for the afternoon patrol. Or in my truck."

He laughed. I just stared at him.

"What patrol? What truck?"

He ignored my questions.

"Come on," he said, moving the barrel of the gun vaguely towards the road. "Up you go."

I put on my jacket and picked up the pack, then clambered up the short bank, trying to hold my jeans up with my other hand. It struck me that I must have lost weight over the last two days. Not eating will do that to you.

On the road I saw a large pick-up truck, parked about fifty metres away. It was facing towards me, and I could see another figure down in the ditch, doing something to the bottom strand of the wire fence.

"So, what we're going to do is walk over to the truck like we're old buddies."

He had walked up next to me, my belt looped around his left wrist, his right hand in his pocket. I saw the barrel of the weapon, which I now realized was a shotgun, coming out from under his jacket and extending parallel to his thigh. He walked on my right, so the gun was away from me, and Badger took up a position on my left.

"Don't try to run away. I won't shoot you, but Badger will sever your hamstrings. He's a hunting dog, brings down at least one pronghorn every fall."

Badger seemed to know he was being talked about. He trotted along but looked up at me with what I could have sworn was a 'go on, try me' grin. I just kept walking between them, down the road. As we approached the truck the person in the ditch came up to the road as well. It was a woman.

"All good," she said. "How's the culvert?"

"It's running clear," my captor said. "There was a small blockage, but I removed it."

They both ignored me. At the truck the woman opened the door on the passenger side, then unlatched the crew cab door as well. I climbed in, the man walking past me and opening the tailgate. Badger jumped up into the back of the truck, the tailgate was slammed shot, and the man came round and got into the drivers' seat. The woman sat in the passenger seat. The truck was started, and we did a slow U-turn in the road, then headed back the way I had walked the day before. My sigh must have been louder than I had intended. The woman laughed softly.

"Sometimes the way forward requires a step back."

Her voice was clear but quiet. The man looked at her sharply.

"I know," she said. "No talking."

We sat in silence for the ten minutes it took us to get to the farm, retracing the two hours it had taken me the day before. The truck pulled into the yard.

"Wait here," the man said. We both stayed where we were. Her hair was blonde, I thought. I don't know what she was thinking. The man opened the front door of the house and went inside. We sat for two or three more minutes. Then he came out, a large cardboard box hugged to his chest. He tipped it over the back of the truck, causing something to slither out of the box.

"It's a tarp," said the woman, not moving her head. The man turned, still holding the box, opened my side door, and told me to get down. The woman got out at the same time, came around to my side of the truck, and held one side of the cardboard box. They walked to the door together, effectively shepherding me in front of them. Badger ran ahead.

We entered the farmhouse and I found myself in a mudroom.

"Take off your boots."

I did that, then was gestured in through a door and into a large kitchen. Badger went and lay down on a rug spread in front of a wood stove, the old-fashioned metal kind with legs and a glass door. A thermal fan on top of the stove turned gently, even though the fire itself had burned down to ashes.

The man and woman came in behind me. She put some wood on the fire, blowing on it gently to coax out a flame, then filled a kettle at the sink and put it next to the fan. He leaned against a counter. I saw that he had the shotgun again, but at least this time it was pointing at the floor.

"So," he said. "Who the hell are you?"

We sat in the kitchen and drank tea while we talked. Evening fell, and at one point the woman got up and switched on the security light in the yard. I told them what I had seen, in Calgary just two days ago, and how I had decided to get back to my wife and daughters. The two of them didn't really understand my motivation, so I tried to explain.

"I'm a teacher," I said, and gave them a brief history. How I had lived and taught on small islands in the Caribbean for nearly a decade, then decided I could be just as useful in Canada and spent about the same amount of time on northern reserves, working with the Cree and Dene peoples. Then leaving one classroom for another, switching from teacher to student as I studied for my doctoral degree before ending up teaching at the university. That had given me the opportunity to do some international development work as well, helping to rebuild the education system in the post-conflict of what used to be Yugoslavia once the smoke cleared from the Balkan wars.

"I've seen occupation in practice," I said, "and one thing I learned is, if you want to get out, you have to get out quick. I've seen the mass graves of people who thought they could stay, that reason would prevail. Do you remember Srebrenica? You should. We all should. You have to start moving and keep moving."

The man looked at me and shook his head.

"You think it'll get that bad? Why? They need us to do the work, to keep everything going."

"No, they don't. Look at East Timor, at Irian Jaya, even at Fiji if you go back far enough. They bring in their own people, from their overcrowded cities, and you end up being a serf class, if you manage to get a job at all. Actually, what has been happening? What have you heard on the news?"

They looked at each other, then the woman spoke.

"The first story was that they were coming because the Premier had asked for help, to separate from central Canada. He denied that, of course, but some of his people said it was true. And a lot of the rural folks quite like the idea, they still remember King Ralph's comment that he was going to let those eastern bastards freeze in the dark. And they don't just remember, they agree."

The man chimed in.

"It was only the next day, when their President went on Twitter and said that now they would have the fresh water and oil and timber they needed, no more of the stupid tariffs which Canada was imposing, that some of us figured maybe this wasn't quite as invitational as we'd been led to believe."

I was astounded.

"But what about the bombings, and the strafing, and the paratroopers," I said. "How invitational was that?"

The man shrugged. "The reports were that there was one incident, a single commander who got a bit carried away, but everything else went well."

The woman spoke. "The news just said that we were being given some help to get things under control. It has been pretty bad, you know. We lost a lot of people in the pandemic, and then the weather has destroyed a lot of farm livelihoods. Crazy storms coming out of nowhere, droughts all summer, huge snowfalls in the winter—everything has been upside down. The oil patch is in a mess because they won't let people drill any more, and the feds keep talking about nuclear power or wind farms instead of getting a pipeline built to take the oil to Canadian refineries in New Brunswick."

"Yeah," said the man, "it's all the fault of Quebec. They want everything to be done in French but don't realize that we're the ones with the resources. They want our tax money but then say everything should be fifty-fifty. It's outrageous."

"What about the border? The one between Manitoba and Ontario. What have you heard about that?"

"Yes, that was closed," he said. "But by the Canadians."

"It was done to keep westerners out," said the woman, "to stop them taking jobs."

"How much sense does that make," I said. "Really? Close the border to keep half the country separated? When all they want is our tax money?"

There was silence in the room. The woman refilled our cups with more tea. The man left the shotgun against the counter and joined us at the table. He took out a pouch of tobacco and some papers, rolled a thin cigarette, lit it, and blew out the smoke.

"No sense at all," he said. "The same way it makes no sense that my neighbour's three sons now drive their jeep along our road each afternoon, one driving, one asking people what they're doing, and the third sitting in the back holding a thirty oh eight deer rifle. The same way that it makes no sense there is some sort of drone patrolling the highway. The same way that it makes no sense that yesterday I got a phone call from somebody, I still don't know who, telling me that my cows somehow got out of a gated pasture and walked across a bridge in the middle of the night. The same way it makes no sense that I find a stranger hiding under the culvert. So, what does make sense, then? Then tell me that."

"Well, bombing universities and airports and strafing civilians doesn't seem a good way to show support or win the hearts and minds of people, does it?"

He laughed. "Not really, no. It's a bit worrying that they've been able to close down the news, though. Did you have cell coverage in the city?"

"I don't know," I said. "I left my phone behind. I made one call but that was on my landline."

"There must be news somewhere," said the woman. "We just haven't looked properly."

"Maybe we should start there?" I said, putting down my cup. "Do you have a computer?"

CHAPTER 5

The woman and I spent the next two hours together. First, we tried the usual social media suspects, but there were no connections. Facebook was "temporarily unavailable in your region", Twitter simply did not seem to exist, and Instagram presented a static image of a goat in a tree. Then we went on the computer, surfing the various news sites and trying to patch together some idea of the situation.

It was a frustrating time. There were some vague references to an 'intervention', and on one renowned right-wing site a call to support those who were trying to bring peace and prosperity back to the province, but that was about it. There were no photographs, no videos, no breathless first-person accounts. It was, in its own way, even more intimidating.

"There was more news out of Homs during the Syrian civil war," I said. "This is nuts."

"Right," said the woman. "Let's go back to the beginning. You said you phoned your wife, right? On your land line?"

"Yes."

"What's the number?"

"Her number?"

"Both of them. And your cell phone."

I told her the numbers and she wrote them down. Then she picked up the phone which was perched in a cradle on the counter.

"Hang on," I said. "If they are blocking communications, then maybe they are tracing calls as well. Do you really want your phone number to be popping up on their screens?"

She looked at me, and then across the room to the man, who had spent the past couple of hours sorting through the canned and dried food on the kitchen shelves, putting some aside and throwing the majority into a large garbage bag. He nodded, apparently in agreement with me.

"He's right. Just give me a minute."

He left the room through one of the connecting doors, heading towards the back of the house. The woman got up from her chair and quickly moved to the counter, leaning against it and making sure that I could see her hand was only inches from the shotgun. I shook my head.

"I'm not going to do anything. I'm on your side, remember."

"Are you? I don't even know who's playing, let alone whose side I'm on."

The man came back in and threw an old Nokia phone on to the table.

"That still works," he said. "At least, I think it does. It's been upstairs plugged in since ... you know."

His voice trailed off. The woman flashed him a sympathetic glance, then picked up the phone.

"OK, we'll try using this. It was our dad's phone, he passed away a couple of weeks ago so it should still have credit. He never wanted a plan, he always bought those pay-as-you-go options. So, this shouldn't be registered to anywhere, except to a dead man."

"Maybe just use it and throw it away," said the man. "Just in case."

I nodded. The woman looked at him but didn't say anything. Then she dialed.

"This first number is your home landline," she said. "We know that was working." She listened to the phone, which seemed to have gone to voice mail.

"We're sorry but this number is no longer in service," she reported. She clicked off the call and then dialled again.

"Your cell phone." She listened. "We're sorry but this customer is currently not available. Hmmm."

She clicked off the phone again and dialed a third time. This time there was no message, simply a loud crackle of static which made all of us wince.

"That was Ontario," she said. "Hey, Dave, grab that feedlot calendar off the wall, does it have any out of province numbers on it?"

He glared at her, obviously mad that she had given away his name, but went to the fridge and pulled the calendar out from under a magnetic cow. He looked quickly at the back.

"Here's the National Union contact number, in Mississauga."

"That'll do," she said, and dialed as he read out the numbers. Once again there was a loud and piercing burst of static.

She clicked off the phone again and sat back down at the table with me. The man was still standing.

"So, you're Dave," I said. "Pleased to meet you. I'm Claude."

He looked at me for a minute, then came over to the

table, shook my hand, and sat down in the third chair. Gesturing over he said, "that's my sister, Jess."

I nodded over to her and she extended her hand, which I shook as well.

"So, don't you normally live here?"

Jess shook her head.

"I live over in Hanna, well close by, we've got a ranch there. My partner and me."

"I live here part-time," said Dave. "I've got a little place in town as well but I'm usually here, helping dad. That's my run-away place."

"Your Sunday morning hang-over place!" laughed Jess.

Dave nodded.

"Who was the fellow who was with you, in the truck, when you came for the cows?" I asked.

"That was Brian, he farms up the road aways. I called him after I got the message about my cows being out of the pasture. Hang on. That means I've made a call on my phone and that was OK. Let me try again."

He pulled his phone out of his pocket and dialled a number from memory. It clicked through, rang, and was quickly answered.

"Oh, hi Brian. I was just thinking, maybe I'll head to Drumheller over the next day or so, drop Jess back up to her place at Hanna. Would you be able to keep an eye on things here, maybe feed Badger? You would? Great. Cheers, I'll let you know when we have a proper plan."

"So, my phone works for local calls," he said, clicking it shut. "Maybe I'll just give Aunt Joanie a quick call, she needs to know about dad. She lives in Fredericton, New Brunswick," he said to me, going over to the fridge and peering at a piece of paper. He found the number he was looking for and dialed it, only to hold the phone away from his ear as the static shrieked again. He came back to the table and sat down.

"Well, it seems we can talk locally but can't connect with anyone in the big city, or out of province. That all sounds a bit strange," he said.

"Strange?" I said. "It's downright scary. What kind of technology can throw a complete blanket over such a wide range of communications? I've seen it before, where cell phones get disrupted when an army convoy goes past. They used that trick in Afghanistan, hoping that it would stop someone triggering an IED as they drove by, but it was limited in range to a couple of blocks. This is almost over a whole province!"

Dave looked at me strangely. "What were you doing in Afghanistan?" he said.

"Oh, that was another project. I did a bit of work with the Ministry of Education there, trying to help them restructure the school system after the war."

"After?" he said. "I thought it was still going on?"

"Well, it is a bit, true. I like to say I was working in a post-conflict context that could have been a bit more post and a bit less conflict. But it was OK."

We sat in silence for a while. At last Jess got to her feet.

"Well," she said. "I think the next thing we should do is go to bed and get some sleep. It's getting late. We can talk about this some more in the morning. Good night to both of you."

She walked out of the room towards the back of the house.

"I'm going to trust you to stay quiet and not do anything stupid," said Dave. "But just to be sure, I'm going to give you a room we usually just use as a pantry."

He got up and walked past the fridge, then down a short

corridor which ended in a door. He opened it and turned on the light. There was a shelving unit along one wall, piled high with cans, and tubs of what looked like peat moss at the base of another wall. A small camp bed stood in the middle of the room, covered in a sheet and what looked like a thick horse blanket. On the floor next to it was a bucket, with a roll of toilet paper next to the bucket. There was no window in the room.

"The door doesn't lock," said Dave, "but I don't want you up and about for two reasons. One, because I want to feel safe when I go to sleep tonight. And two, because Badger is going to be sleeping right outside your door and I don't want him to hurt you if you decide to go walkabout. We'll go back to the kitchen now, you can get your bag and a jug of water if you want, then you're in here until Jess or me come by in the morning."

It wasn't said as a suggestion or a possibility, and I didn't argue. I went with him and got my bag, and an empty glass as well as the jug of water, and took my stuff into the small room.

"One thing," I said, as he started to leave. "Can I leave the door open a little bit? I won't go out of the room, but I get a bit claustrophobic, I don't know I want to be shut in here with the door closed."

Dave thought for a moment.

"The dog will have you if you step outside," he reiterated.

"I won't. Promise."

"OK, then, leave it open a crack."

Taking the shotgun, he walked away, turning off the lights as he left. My light spilled out a bit into the corridor, and I could see Badger spreading himself across the width of the floor. He looked at me and gave me that smile again.

"Good night, Badger," I said, and got myself ready for bed.

When I woke up, I was still in the middle of my dream. I'd been walking through a dark forest and slipped down a narrow embankment to a creek, where my feet became trapped in thick mud. As much as I tried to lift them out, they wouldn't move. My boots were sucked off and I could feel twigs and leaves pressing into my ankles. Even as I opened my eyes, I could still feel the weight of the mud, pressing down on me.

I lifted my head a fraction and looked down the bed. Badger lay across the bottom of my blanket, fast asleep. I moved my foot a little, trying to ease it out from under his weight, and he opened one eye. His tailed wagged, once, then he closed his eye and went back to sleep.

I slowly wriggled my feet out from under him, at which point he gave a loud sigh, stood up on the bed, and looked directly at me. He then turned around a couple of times, scratched at the blanket with his paw, then lay down again. This time he was up against my leg, but not on it, so there was no feeling of being trapped. But I knew that I could not move. Indeed, when I tried to edge sideways a little, so that I wasn't touching him, Badger opened his eye and stared at me again until I put my leg back in the original position. Then he went back to sleep.

I lay there for another hour before I heard footsteps above me. A toilet flushed, and then suddenly the door opened, and Dave was standing there. He switched on the light.

"Well, don't you two look cozy," he said.

"Can I get up now?"

He gave the same short whistle and Badger jumped down off the camp bed, albeit reluctantly.

"Bathroom is free," said Dave. "Jess is making coffee."

I followed him to the back of the house, where he left me to make my ablutions. The bathroom was a normal sort of bathroom, with a shower over the bathtub and a cracked glass mirror on the vanity.

There was the normal assortment of pills old guys use, to help them sleep or to smooth their aches and pains, and a new razor still in its hard plastic wrap. I pulled it out and yelled out to Dave to ask if I could use it. He agreed, so I lathered up and had a shave. When I had finished and came out of the bathroom, Badger was sitting outside the door, then preceded me down the corridor back to the kitchen. I sat at the table and Badger sat close by my leg.

"He likes you," said Jess, bringing me over a mug of coffee. "Milk and creamer are there, "she said, pointing at a bowl in the middle of the table, "and Dave might leave you some sugar."

He grunted, pushing over another bowl and a spoon.

"It's OK, black's good for me," I said. Then I tasted the coffee. I reached for the sugar. Dave laughed.

"It's Jess's special farmhouse blend," he said. "Kind of on the wake-you-up side."

"Toast?" said Jess. We both agreed that would be a good idea, and soon a plate of hot toast was in front of us, together with some raspberry jam, and a jar of peanut butter. Jess joined us at the table, and the three of us ate without talking. When he had finished his two slices of toast, Dave took out his tobacco pouch and rolled a cigarette. He offered the pouch and papers to me, but I shook my head. He lit his smoke, took another slurp of his coffee, then looked over at me.

"So, I've been thinking," he said. Jess and I looked at him expectantly.

"You have this crazy idea you're going to be some sort of new-age fur trader and find your way home to Ontario. Through the bush. On your own. Well, it's your life, and I'm not going to be the one to tell you that you're nuts. You'll work that out all be yourself. But right now you're here, disrupting our lives. My life, anyway."

He looked across at Jess.

"You know I don't want to run this farm," he said. "Now dad's gone, we might as well sell it, plus the stock, and get on with things. You're busy up in Hanna, and I'd like to make things work in town. Are we agreed on that?"

She looked at him with sad eyes. "Yes," she said, "even though it's not what dad would have wanted."

"Yeah, I know. But I don't want to be a farmer, never have. I've got a part time job in the bookstore and coffee shop in town, it could be full time but for me having to be here. I'd much rather be doing that."

I tried to keep my surprise from showing. The idea of this grizzled older guy being more comfortable in a book shop just hadn't been something I had considered. He saw my face and laughed.

"I know, weird isn't it?" he said. "I did a BA in Philosophy and have my masters in English Lit. I love books, love reading them, love the feel of them. I'm even trying to write my own."

"And he's had a couple of short stories published," said Jess, proudly, "plus a book of poems."

"But once mum died, then dad needed help here," said Dave. "So, I helped. He knew that it wasn't my first choice of work, but he thought that I'd come around, that I'd take over from him and run the farm when he wasn't able to do the hard graft. But now here we are."

"Here we are," said Jess, softly.

There was another pause, a different kind of silence this time. Not watchful, more pensive and reflective. Eventually I cleared my throat.

"You said you were thinking something," I said.

"Yes."

Dave stubbed out his cigarette, then got up from the table. He went to the sink and brought back the coffee pot. He filled his and Jess's mugs, I declined. He returned the pot to the stove, then sat down again.

"So, here's the thing," he said. "Like I said to Brian on the phone, I have to take Jess back up to Hanna in the next day or so. We could take you with us and drop you off somewhere like Endiang. That's north of Hanna aways, the other side of Dry Island Buffalo Jump."

He could see that the detail wasn't very helpful, so he got up again, and this time returned with a road map of the province.

"We're here," he said, pointing at the place where the Didsbury road crossed the highway. "This road runs out to Hanna, it goes through Drumheller first, see?"

I nodded. I had my bearings back now.

"I think we can detour up a little and still not raise any suspicions," he said, "and drop you up on the 855 around here somewhere." He pointed to the stretch of road between Hanna and Endiang. "You'll still be about two hundred klicks south of the river, but it's a straight road."

"And what is it to Hanna? About the same?"

"Yeah. Just under. About one seventy, one seventy-five."

"That would be great," I said. "It would be a big chunk out of my route."

Dave nodded. Then he cleared his throat a little, as if he had something else to say.

"There's just one thing," he said.

Jess and I both looked at him.

"What's that?" I said.

"Well, if I move full-time into my place in town, and Jess goes home to Hanna, then what are we going to do about Badger?"

The dog heard his name and sat up, ears perked.

"I thought you'd asked Brian to look after him," I said.

"Well yeah, but that would only be for a couple of days. He's got his own dogs, as does Jess, and Badger doesn't much like company."

I leaned over and scratched the dogs' ears.

"He seems OK with me," I said.

"Well, that's what I was thinking," said Dave. "How about you take him with you, on your trip? It would be safer for you to have a guard dog with you, that's pretty wild country up there. And he'd be company, someone you can talk to and share your crazy stories."

Jess laughed. The dog looked at me. I wasn't sure if it was the right decision, but it was the only possible one, and it was made quickly.

"Sure," I said.

CHAPTER 6

THE NEXT COUPLE of days were busy. Jess and Dave wanted to finish sorting out their dad's stuff, deciding what to keep and what to let go. They gave me odd jobs to do around the farm, and so Badger and I spent our time feeding cows and sweeping out sheds.

In the evenings we talked about what might be happening in the south, in the big cities. Once a neighbour came by, I was in the barn so stood quietly by the door. Dave whistled for Badger, who stood next to him and Jess as they talked with the visitor. I stayed out of sight.

The neighbour said that he'd just been in Edmonton, and things there were quiet. The provincial government was basically doing what it was told and was not pushing back against the newcomers. Their soldiers were all over the city and people generally ignored them. The main highways were still being patrolled but as long as you had a pass you were OK.

"Where did you get the pass?" Dave asked.

"At the council office in Red Deer." The neighbour spat on the ground. "It's like getting a driver's licence. You turn up and show ID, tell them you're a farmer and need to travel around, and they give you a pass with your name on it. Here, look."

He showed a sheet of paper. From my vantage point I could see that it was a simple printed form, with a signature and a stamp from the Reeve.

"They're going to get regular cards printed but they're not ready yet," he said.

"I'll have to go and get one, I guess," said Dave. "I'm going to be taking Jess back over to Hanna later this week."

"You might be OK on our roads," said the neighbour. "I only got stopped once and that was on the four lane."

Dave decided it was better to have a pass, though, so after the neighbour left he took his truck and drove into Red Deer. Jess kept packing boxes, and I carried them from various rooms out to the main kitchen. We had nearly finished when Dave got back. He showed us the pass. Then he looked at me.

"Are you thinking what I'm thinking?"

"You mean, forge another one for me?" I said.

"Yes. It shouldn't be too hard."

"Do you have a printer?"

Jess laughed.

"Of course. Any farm these days is a business, it's all bloody paperwork."

She glanced at the paper.

"That wouldn't be too hard to copy at all. We might have to hand draw the county seal but other than that, no problem."

"The only problem would be if they want to double check the pass against my other ID, you know, something with a photograph on it."

"That's true," Dave said, "but you might be able to bluff

your way out. Say you thought only the pass was needed, and you'll bring your ID to show them later. Something like that."

"And at least you'll have more of a chance than if you didn't have anything," said Jess.

We made up the fake pass that evening, and I folded it over a few times before putting it in my inside pocket of my jacket. My wallet I moved to the very bottom of my backpack. That night Dave brought out a bottle of rum that he found in a cupboard.

"It's Goslings Black Seal," he said. "From Bermuda. My dad got a taste for it when he went down there on holiday one year. Ever since it's been the only drink he'll touch, apart from the odd glass of wine. He used to put ginger beer in it."

"Ginger beer?" I said. "Why?"

"They call it a Dark and Stormy," said Jess, laughing. "There's probably some in the pantry. I'll have a look. I'll get some ice as well."

She came back a few minutes later with some small glass bottles and a tray of ice cubes.

"Here we go. Jamaican Spicy Ginger Beer. Dave, will you do the honours?"

Dave put three ice cubes into each of three glasses, then poured a good slug of the rum over them. Jess went to the drawer and returned with a bottle opener, clipped one of the bottles, and added the fizzy liquid. The glasses were handed around.

I sniffed mine tentatively and immediately started sneezing.

"Wow, that's sharp!" I said. Jess laughed.

"That's the ginger. You get used to it. It's not a fine wine, no need to savour the bouquet. Just drink it!"

So, I did, and found the second sip better than the first, and the third even better. They asked me whether I had ever been to Bermuda, which I had not.

Jess got quite animated and bright eyed as she spoke about her dad and his stories. He had gone back for other visits, apparently, and after their mother had passed, he had talked about spending half the year there, to get away from the Alberta winter.

"He never did, though," said Jess, sadly. "I always told him he had to seize opportunities as they arose, not pass them by and see if they came back later. But he wouldn't leave the cows, not even when Dave said he'd run the place for a couple of months. He just got too stubborn."

We refilled the glasses a few times, and it was after eleven when we finished the bottle and called it quits. I went to my small bedroom and got myself comfortable. Badger climbed on to the mattress after me and curled up by my feet. I clicked off the light. I suppose some part of me wondered whether Jess would come down to the storeroom during the night, but she didn't. I wasn't sure what I felt about that.

WE LEFT EARLY the next morning, my sixth day on the road. Badger and I were crammed into the crew cab of the truck, along with my backpack, while the tray was filled with cardboard boxes. They were covered in a blue tarp held down by bungee cords stretched from corner to corner.

"It's dad's stuff that I don't want to throw out," said Jess, although she didn't really need to explain anything to me. I was only a peripheral part of this family and would soon disappear from their lives.

The journey was pretty straight forward. We chugged along without incident, not seeing any troops or checkpoints or special patrols or anything. It took less than two hours for us to reach Hanna and then swing out on one of the small roads that climbed up on the prairie. Huge fields of some kind of cereal crop stretched as far as one could see.

The badlands were all around us, long deep trenches carved millennia ago and now a veritable treasure trove of dinosaur bones and other prehistoric relics. We wound along a ridge for ten or fifteen minutes, past more grain fields and a couple of fenced in paddocks. One held a dozen or so cattle, the other about the same number of horses.

We left the main road and took a gravelled track to the left, which swung around a bend and then dropped down to a slightly lower terrace.

Here was a house, a low-slung rancher with a long verandah that stretched from end to end. The roof was designed as an overhang, no doubt to both block the sun and also catch any rain which decided to fall. Dave parked the truck up next to a small barn and we climbed down, then followed Jess as she walked across the yard and up the three steps to the deck. A dog barked loudly from somewhere behind the house.

"Hello, I'm home!" she called. The door opened and a woman came out. She looked to be a bit older than Jess, and was more strongly built, but she carried herself with the grace of a dancer. She threw out her arms and they embraced, then Jess turned to face us.

"You know Dave, of course," she said, "and this is Claude. He's just passing through, but I thought I'd bring him by to say hello. Claude, this is my partner, Beverley."

I walked up to her and shook the outstretched hand.

"Pleased to meet you, Beverley," I said.

"Likewise." She looked at me shrewdly, then turned to Dave.

"Hiya big guy, you brought my partner back safe and sound I see!"

"Wouldn't have it any other way," he laughed.

Jess laughed as well, then said, "I'll just put the coffee on," and walked into the house.

At this point Badger came bounding up the steps, tail wagging furiously, and then screeched to a halt in front of Beverley. He sat down and looked straight up at her face.

"Ha, they let you come and visit as well!" she said. "Now let me see ..."

She dug around in the front pocket of her jeans and pulled something out.

"Look what I found," she said, sending Badger almost delirious with delight. His whole body was vibrating, even though he didn't physically move from his spot on the floor. She reached down and held out an open hand, but it wasn't until she said "eat" that he took the morsel from her outstretched palm.

"Crack for dogs," she said, looking across at me. "It's some kind of dried moose and beef jerky that a neighbour makes, and Badger here thinks it's the best food in the world." She tousled his ears, then came to stand next to me.

"Turn around," she said.

I was a bit confused but did as she asked. I was struck silent by what I could see in front of me.

"Wow," I said. Eventually.

THE VIEW from the deck was phenomenal. The terrace extended about 20 metres from the front of the house and then dropped away into a steep sided valley, almost a canyon, which ran at right angles across the landscape. The valley floor was grey and dusty, low tussocks of gravel and clumps of some kind of shrub dotted across the otherwise barren landscape.

A dirt road wound its serpentine way through the impediments, the surface showing vehicle tracks. The opposite side of the valley was perhaps a kilometre away, concertinaed bands of rock, each one a different shade of many colours—red, white, brown, black. It looked like someone had taken a layer cake and gently pressed it inwards from the edges, so the layers remained distinct but no longer horizontal.

"Pretty cool, uh?" said Beverley.

I just shook my head.

"It's amazing." A thought struck me. "What direction are we looking, across the valley?"

"We're looking pretty much due east," she said. "Straight at the sunrise."

I just stood there. Eventually I turned to her.

"What an incredible place to live," I said.

Beverley smiled. "Indeed."

"How big is your property?" I asked.

I had some awareness of the scale of things in rural Alberta but even so, I was unprepared for the response.

"There's six quarter sections of land altogether. The home quarter around here, with the house, another two quarters of pasture up on the ridge, and then three quarters down there in the valley. Pretty much all you can see. Just under a thousand acres in all," she said.

"A thousand acres?"

I figured that the house in Calgary was on a large lot, but that was less than one third of an acre.

"Yes. Each section is planned out to be one square mile in size, which works out to six hundred and forty acres. Each quarter section is obviously one hundred and sixty acres, and we have six of those. That's a bit less than the average size for an Alberta ranch these days, but it's big enough for us. Isn't it, Jess?"

Jess nodded. She had come out behind me and now she handed us each a cup of coffee. Dave wandered out with another two cups, one of which he gave to his sister. We all stood quietly for a moment, then Jess indicated some roughly hewn logs arranged around a small fire pit.

"Let's sit," she said. "Claude, you go on that side, so you can enjoy the view."

We all moved across and sat down. Dave pulled out his tobacco pouch and rolled a cigarette. He offered me the pouch, but I shook my head. He lit up, then breathed out a great sigh.

"Pretty spectacular, isn't it?" he said.

"It sure is," I agreed. I looked across at Jess. "So, what do you do here? Do you grow stuff? I mean, you can't grow anything down there, can you?" I indicated to the valley.

"Good question," she said. "No, we can't grow anything down there, as you put it. What we have here is mainly a grain operation, but we don't actually farm it ourselves. I lease the two quarter sections up on the top to a farmer from over Oyen way, he crops it on a seven-year rotation that we both agreed was best. We're coming to the end of the second rotation and so far, things have worked out pretty well."

"The rules are a bit different out here," said Beverley. "We're in what's called a Special Area Zone, so there are special regulations. A lot of the land around us is not privately owned any more."

"For example," said Jess, "most of the land we saw after

we left Hanna was last farmed in the nineteen thirties. Then there was the great drought, the depression, the dust bowl, call it what you like, and a lot of folks just got up and walked away, leaving everything. By the late thirties there were very few people left and the banks owned a lot of land that they had no way of using."

"So as a result," said Beverley, "the government set up this Special Areas Act and appointed a board to look after the land. They set up community pastures and charged people a fee to graze their cattle, that sort of thing. But they also made this rule that you can't break any undisturbed or uncultivated land, any of the old prairie."

"Even though it had mostly already been broken in the late eighteen hundreds," muttered Dave.

"Well, we don't know that, actually," said Beverley, tartly. "So, there's lots of original prairie up there and we drove past some of it. In some places, you can still see the ruts made by the wagon trains of the early settlers, when they came out here at the turn of the century."

"1909," said Jess. "That's when the first settler came."

"But you and your farmer friend can grow crops?" I asked. "You can cultivate? Why is that? Why are the rules different for you?"

The women both laughed.

"No," said Jess, "we are OK because our land was cultivated by one of the early settlers, a fellow from the Dakotas who came here in about nineteen fourteen. Local legend says he only left the property twice. Once he went to Edmonton for a weekend and when he came back, he had a wife. The second time was when they all disappeared, him and his wife and his four kids, one night in nineteen thirty-six. Nobody knows if they went to the city, or back to the

States, or simply walked out into the coulee and died out there."

"Coulee?" I asked.

"What you called the valley," said Beverley. "Its proper name is a coulee."

"Anyway," said Jess, "back to the story. Because he had broken the land, we are allowed to cultivate it as well. We've been here fifteen years now, and so we have a good arrangement. Josef, the farmer, he keeps the rotation going. We have two years of cereal, then field peas, cereal again, canola, another cereal, and then a year of fallow. The cereals change depending on market conditions and stuff, but are things like wheat, oats, barley. Right now, it's barley."

"We've also got a couple of paddocks that you might have seen just before you came off the ridge," said Beverley.

"Right," I said. "One had cows in it, the other had horses."

Beverley laughed. "Steers. Not cows. A steer is a neutered bullock, we raise them just for their meat. We get them when they're about six months old and then let them run in the pasture for eighteen months, then they go off to the abattoir. Because they're grass fed and free range, we get a good price for them, usually at least three or four dollars a pound extra compared to the ones coming from the feedlots down by Lethbridge."

"The horses are for the other part of our business," said Jess. "In the summer we run tourists out into the coulee, for adventure breaks. Some of them want to look for fossils, some are bird watchers or plant hunters or whatever, some just want to admire the scenery. We take them out and around and have built a small tipi down in the back quarter, next to the river. We cook them a meal and light the fire, and they camp the night there. One of us always stays close by as well, to make sure they don't do something foolish."

"Like what?"

"It varies," said Beverley. "Early on, we had one fellow get completely smashed on some rye he'd brought with him, he started getting all aggressive towards one of the women in the group. Other times we've had people trying to commune with nature, they smoke dope or eat mushrooms or whatever, then go wandering around the place. And it can be dangerous."

"Can it?" I said. "In what ways?"

"Well," said Dave, "you've got rattlers for a start, and scorpions. Then there are coyotes as well. So, if you fall off a hoodoo and are lying there helpless, you've got no chance."

"That's true," said Jess. "But it's more likely you might slip and fall and break something, or else go into the river. So, we just try to unobtrusively take care of our guests. They have a nice ride out in the coulee, a meal, campfire, a night in a tent or under the stars, and then a leisurely ride back up here the next day. Five hundred bucks, all inclusive, and we have an old milk churn we leave as a tip jar."

"Each?" I said.

"Yes, although if it's a couple who are going to share a tent then we give them a hundred dollar discount, so it's nine hundred for two. We usually get that lost hundred back as a tip. We only take up to six or seven people on each trip, and only run them twice a week during the summer, so there's a bit of a line up for people wanting to have the experience. So, that's all good." Jess set her coffee cup down.

"You should stay here tonight," she said. "Then tomorrow we'll get you on your way."

Dave looked at her, questioningly. "Do you want me to stay?"

"Not unless you want to," she said. "I think we can manage."

He nodded.

"Right then, I'll unload the truck and then get on my way," he said.

"I'll give you a hand," I said. We left the two women by the firepit and went over to the truck.

"Unhook the ties, will you?" said Dave. He went on to the barn and opened the door, then came back to me and pulled down the tailgate.

"You pass them down and I'll put them away," he said. "I kind of know where they're going."

"OK," I said, and started lifting the boxes. There were about thirty of them, and each had to be taken down, walked across into the garage, and restacked, so it took us nearly an hour. Now and then I looked across and saw that Jess and Beverley were in deep conversation.

"Talking about you, I expect," said Dave, when he saw me glancing over in that direction.

"Don't worry, they'll see you right."

Once we'd finished, there was still one carton left in the truck. Dave carried it as we walked back over to the women. He put the box on the steps and wiped his hands on the legs of his jeans.

"All done," he said. "I've tried to keep things in some sort of order, Jess. Book boxes in one pile, tools in another, clothes in a third, that sort of thing. This here box is the booze we packed, the left over bottles."

"Thanks, Dave," she said. "You too, Claude, that was a great help".

I nodded. Dave turned to me.

"I'll leave Badger with you. Claude, good luck, hope things work out for you."

We shook hands.

"Cheers."

He waved, then walked over to the truck and climbed inside. He started it up, then with another wave drove slowly up the narrow track and up to the prairie. We heard him accelerate as he got on to the black top, but soon the sounds of the engine died away. The three of us looked at each other.

"Time for some lunch, I think," said Beverley, and we went into the house. I carried the box into the front room and unpacked it, stacking the bottles as directed in a small liquor cabinet. I was surprised to see a full bottle of black rum, as well some more of the ginger beer, in addition to the various bottles of wine.

CHAPTER 7

As I had expected, lunch was a bit of an interrogation. Beverley was catching up and expanding on some of the things Jess had told her while Dave and I were unloading the truck, and she wanted to hear it in my own words. We went over what I had seen, and why I was on the road, and where I was going, and she probed for details if she thought I was being unclear. But I did manage to pose some questions of my own and found out more about the region.

"This place is right in Palliser's triangle," said Beverley. "Have you heard of that?"

"A little," I said. "Wasn't he a surveyor or something, for the British government, back in the day? I thought he said you couldn't grow anything in it, in his triangle that is."

"Well, sort of. He was a captain in the British Army and wrote a report for the government, yes. But he came through here in the eighteen fifties and found the whole area to be unsuitable for agriculture. The triangle goes from up near Edmonton down to the US border, then across to southern Manitoba, and back via Saskatoon to Edmonton—the

Yellowhead Highway pretty much follows the long edge of the triangle."

"The hypotenuse," said Jess.

"Indeed," said Beverley, "I knew you doing math at high school would come in useful one day. Anyway, Captain Palliser came here during a dry spell, there was no rain, there were grass fires all over the place, and he wasn't impressed. But then thirty years later another expedition came by and it happened to be a wet spell, so there was lots of grass and flowers and so on, and they wrote a report saying the prairie was beautiful and ripe for development. Guess which report the government followed?"

"And that's when they opened up the prairies for settlement?" I said.

"Pretty much, although like I said, that didn't really take off until the turn of the century."

"Then in the thirties," said Jess, "folks agreed that maybe Palliser was right all along."

"Yes," said Beverley. "Even now, we can count on about ten inches of rain a year, and about four feet of snow. Now if the rain comes at the right time, and the snow melts gently over a couple of weeks and not through one single chinook, then maybe there'll be enough moisture in the ground for a crop."

"Do you irrigate?"

"No, we get our water from the well," said Jess, "and there are a couple of small artesian wells to give water to the animals. But the aquifer isn't big enough for the major irrigation systems you see in other parts of Alberta. So, we rely a bit on mother nature."

"Luckily there's not a big population," said Beverley. "Even with the towns like Hanna and Oyen and Consort counted in, there's only about one person every thousand acres. Some folks call this the Empty Quarter, kind of like that desert in Saudi Arabia."

"Nobody has mentioned the Blackfoot yet," said Jess, raising her finger in admonishment. "This was all the traditional land of the Confederacy. Even now when we're out walking, we sometimes come across arrow heads, and I'm convinced that there's one place in the coulee where they had a buffalo jump. A couple of provincial people came out to have a look, they said it has got all the right, what would you call them, attributes? There's a flat area of prairie that kind of slopes down to the top of the coulee, and there is a natural gulley that would help them channel the buffalo down and over the edge. The cliff, well it's not really a cliff, just a ten-metre drop, but it is pretty vertical, and the ground underneath is fairly level as well. And there's a small spring and a pool not too far away, in the coulee itself, which would make a great camp site. From my reading, those are all things which are needed."

I nodded.

"Yes, that sounds about right. I went down to Head Smashed In once, by the Chain Lakes south of Kananaskis country, they've got a great museum there and it tells the story. You're lucky to have that."

"Well, it's not really ours," send Beverley. "They told us that it would be protected as a Provincial Heritage Resource or something, so we are not allowed to disturb anything. One day they might have money to develop it. We figure we're the ones tasked with looking after it right now. So, we just do what we can. More coffee?"

She poured me another cup from the percolator, then sat back in her chair and looked at me. I got the feeling that she was about to say something important. Jess stood up from the table and collected our plates.

"Just a sec," she said, walking out into the kitchen. Beverley and I just looked at each other. I heard a flurry of squawks from outside, one bird much louder than the other, then things quietened down again.

"Stupid chickens," said Jess, returning to the table with a plate of cookies. "We've got half a dozen, just for the eggs really, although they are nice to look at as well. Which is good, as they're otherwise expensive eggs, what with the special chicken scratch we have to feed them to supplement what they can find around the place."

She sat down, pushing the cookies over towards me. Badger didn't move from his place on the floor next to my feet, but his ears perked up.

"No thanks, I'm good," I said, taking my coffee cup in hand. Badger drooped his ears again. I waited.

At last Beverley leaned forward, putting down her cup. She glanced across at Jess, who nodded, then returned her attention to me.

"So," she said, "when you were washing up, before lunch, Jess and me were chatting, and we've had an idea. You don't have to say yes, but I would like you to hear me out, OK?"

"Sure," I said, interested in spite of myself.

"Well, we know you're wanting to head north and get to the river, but this isn't a good time to be doing that. The water will be low and it will be difficult paddling, lots of shoals. Plus, it's still summer, the kids aren't back in school yet, so there will be lots of people out and about. So basically, you can go if you want to, and that's fine, but we think you should stay here for a couple of weeks."

I hadn't expected that.

"Really?" I said. "That's very kind ..."

Jess broke in.

"It would help us as well," she said. "This is always a busy time and we could use an extra set of hands. It would give you a chance to follow the news a bit, and maybe change your plans if needed. There seems to be a lot more news now, more than when we tried the other night to find out what was happening."

That had only been four days ago, I realized, and it was less than a week since I'd left Calgary.

"So, what's the deal?" I said.

BEVERLEY LAID things out quite succinctly, with Jess throwing in a comment every now and again. In essence, it seemed that Josef the farmer would soon be cropping the grain, and as part of his rent he always dropped twenty bales of hay down to the coulee below the farm. This, properly supplemented with oats, provided winter feed for the cattle and the horses. But it had to be moved and stored in the barn, and then the animals had to be brought down from the high prairie.

"They could probably survive up there," said Jess, "but we have to be out twice a day to check on them. It's easier if they're down in the coulee. The winds aren't as bad down there, and the drifts aren't too bad either. So, we round them up and walk them down. You haven't seen the barn down there, it's a good size and there's lots of shelter."

"I also think you need more information," said Beverley, "I really do. Things seem to be going totally sideways in the big cities, and I heard that there is a lot of tension between the west and the rest of Canada. I don't think you know enough about what's happening, none of us do."

"That's right," said Jess. "We're kind of out of the way

here, but that also means that everyone would notice a strange guy walking up the road or hitching a ride in my truck. I'm expecting someone to drop by any time, actually. They'll say they need to borrow some engine oil or something, but really the grapevine will have told them that I came back with Dave and another feller, and Dave left on his own."

"Really? People are that nosey, even way out here?"

"They sure are," said Jess. "You just watch. But if you're working here then we can just say you're a field hand we've hired on for a couple of weeks, there's lots of guys who travel around providing casual farm labour. That would give you some cover, even if you never leave the property. When Josef drops by, for example, or someone comes to see if we want the septic pumped out or whatever, there's a reason you're here."

"Wouldn't they phone?" I said.

"Out here? No." Beverley laughed. "People come for a visit whenever they can, otherwise they're just sitting in an office all day. Everyone would rather be in their truck, driving the back roads, looking for pronghorn. It's amazing how many people manage to always have a bit of venison in the freezer. So no, people will likely drop in, and you won't have to hide, just be working."

It didn't take long for me to make up my mind and accept the offer. Jess stayed in the house to clean up the lunch stuff, while Beverley took Badger and me out to the barn. An old pick-up truck with rust lines through the paint was parked in the shadows.

"That's the farm truck," said Beverley. "We use it for hauling stuff around the property, and the odd trip to town."

As we walked past the corner of the house I heard barking again.

"We've got a couple of guard dogs," said Beverley, "but they're not too good with people. Or with other dogs."

She leaned down and scratched Badger's ears.

"Anyway, we have a pen set up behind the house, and they stay there. Out of sight, but always around. You can check them out if you like but don't take Badger."

"Maybe later," I said. We kept walking.

Once we got to the barn we navigated between the piles of boxes and then, in the gloom at the back, I realized that there were some steps. We went up them and came out into an open space.

"This is our hired hand space," said Beverley. I looked around. The stairs had brought us up into a large spacious room.

"This used to be the hay loft," said Beverley, "but we converted it a few years back."

The walls came up about three feet and then angled inwards towards a flat ceiling. The room extended the length of the barn, the floor bare wood planks that had been sanded down to a soft sheen. There were three skylights along each side, and at the end there was a large glass door.

As we walked through the room, I realized that the furniture was organized in clusters.

"We've set it up so there's a sleeping space and a kind of work space, and a relaxing space," she said, as we walked past first a large bed, then a small desk, and then at the end a large sectional settee and two armchairs. There was a small wood stove at that end as well, with a chimney that went up vertically and then angled out to the side before exiting through the wall. We reached the glass door and Beverley opened it.

As we stepped through the door, I suddenly realized that this led into a small balcony, sheltered from the elements by the two gables of the barn and with a low balustrade at the end. There was just room for two wooden Adirondack chairs, one painted bright red and the other a canary yellow, with a metal ashtray on a stand between them. The view was out across the coulee.

"Towards the dawn," said Beverley, smiling at the look on my face.

"I don't know what to say," I said. "It's absolutely fantastic."

"Well, it's really pretty basic," she said. "But people seem to find it OK for short stays."

We walked back into the main room and headed back towards the steps. She pointed to a wall that rose behind the opening to the stairs, and a small door to the side.

"Behind there is a simple toilet and shower room," she said. "There's also a kettle in case you want to make a cup of tea or anything, but you'll eat meals with us. That's basically your pay, minimum wage plus room and board. Fifteen bucks an hour for what we say is an eight-hour day, even though some days are longer than others. OK?"

"Sure," I said.

"Breakfast is at seven each morning, up at the house, and lunch is when we can grab it. We try and wrap up the day by five or so, then have a quiet hour before dinner at six thirty. After dinner you're free to do as you wish. If you want to wash clothes, then there's a line along the other side of the barn and you can hang them out to dry there."

"Can Badger stay with me?"

"Of course." She leaned down and ruffled his ears. "He's a good dog to have around. Let's get your bag."

Just then we heard the noise of an engine as a vehicle changed gears and started down the road to the terrace. We went back down the stairs and out to the yard. An old Ford

F-150 came into view and pulled up next to us. The window slid down and a grizzled face looked out. He wore a green John Deere hat and had an unlit cigarette behind his ear.

"Afternoon Bevvy," said the old man, nodding at me in nonchalant fashion. "Just checking to see how your septic's doing. See whether it needs emptying out yet?"

Beverley gave a choking cough but recovered swiftly.

"No, I think it's fine, Henry," she said. "It's not been even three months since you were last here. You said it would be OK for another year."

"Aye, but that was based on just two of you'se using it," he said, looking at me again, a bit more meaningfully this time. I just smiled at him.

Beverley shook her head, trying to keep a straight face.

"We've not had anyone else here except for me and Jess," she said, "and her brother Dave the odd night. Now we've got Claude here to give us a ... oh, I'm sorry. I guess you won't have met."

She gestured at me to step forward.

"Henry, let me introduce you to Claude, our new hired hand. He was working at the farm with Jess's dad and stayed to help Dave while everything was happening."

I saw Henry surreptitiously cross himself. Beverley noticed as well.

"Yes, it was an awful shock. You must pay your respects to Jess while you're here. Anyway, Dave has decided to sell the farm now, so Jess invited Claude to come and work for us for a few weeks, before he moves on."

Beverley half turned to me.

"Claude, this is Henry, he lives up on the prairie to the east aways, nearly to Consort actually. We use his services whenever we need the septic tank pumped out."

I nodded at Henry, again, and stuck out my arm to shake hands. Henry reached out of the cab and gripped my hand in his. He looked at me.

"Soft hands for a farmhand," he said.

"I try to wear gloves a lot," I said. It was all I could think of at the time, and I was glad I was wearing a long-sleeved shirt, so he couldn't see the telltale lack of sunburned skin extending all the way up my arm.

"Aye then." He held my hand a bit longer than comfortable, then let go and looked back to Beverley.

"Is Jess around, Bevvy?"

"Yes, she is. Jess!" she shouted, but Jess must have heard the truck arrive and was already walking down the steps and across the yard.

"Henry's here to check on the septic, Jess," said Beverley, looking everywhere but at her partner, who kept her gaze steadily on the old man. "I'll leave you with him, I was just going to show Claude his space. See you later, Henry."

She started walking away from the truck, back towards the barn.

"Nice meeting you, Henry," I said, and followed her across the yard, grabbing my bag from the cab of the truck as we passed. Once we were inside the barn Beverley closed the door and almost ran up the stairs. I followed her at a more leisurely pace and found her in the small kitchenette, leaning against the wall. She was holding her face in her hands, tears streaming down her cheeks, and shaking with laughter.

"Oh ... my ... God," she gasped, when at last she could speak. "Jess so called that! Didn't she say someone would come around to check the septic? Didn't she?"

She crumpled up in laughter again. I left her and walked down the long room to the glass door, looking out without opening it. Jess was just waving as Henry slowly turned his old truck in a big semicircle and then cruised back up the hill. I went back to Beverley, who had more or less composed herself.

"He's just gone," I said.

Beverley nodded, her eyes still sparkling from her tears.

"Right. Well, let me go and see how Jess coped with that. You can have a quiet hour now. Get yourself sorted. Then come down to the house around four and we'll go down to the coulee, we can show you around down there."

I looked at my watch as she moved away. It was just after three. She went down the steps and Badger followed me as I went back into the main room.

It did not take me long to unpack my few things. I took off my old clothes and had a shower, washing my shirt and underwear out in the sink as I did so. Once I had dried off, I put on my clean gear, then hunted around until I found some pegs in a cloth bag under the sink. I carried my newly cleaned clothes downstairs and pegged them out on the line, which was strung between the corner post of the barn and a nearby poplar.

Then I went back upstairs and put on the kettle. There were some tea bags in a small tin, so I took one and put it in a mug with a Stettler Steam Railway slogan proudly emblazoned upon it, even if it was somewhat worn. I took the tea and checked the small fridge, but there was no milk, so I took it black. Then I went out to the balcony.

I sat there quietly, sipping my tea and watching the play of the light on far slopes of the coulee. Badger lay by my feet. The sun was still high in the mid-afternoon sky and so there were not the intricate shadows and highlights which I knew would come later. Instead, the impression was almost two dimensional.

There were the subdued greys and whites of the coulee floor, then the squashed lines of the layer cake rocks topped with a thin green line and then the azure blue sky. As an image it was reminiscent of a Rothko design executed by Hockney, complex in structure but clear in expression, and very pleasing to the eye.

A couple of weeks here would not hurt, I thought to myself. Beverley was right when she spoke about the schools not being back in class yet, and if I got to do some physical labour then that would no doubt stand me in good stead for the days ahead. If I was being paid as well then that was even better, as it would give me a bit more cash for the journey.

And to wake up to this view every morning, that was an unexpected bonus. All in all, this could be a win-win, I thought. I finished my tea and walked back inside. Badger stayed on the balcony while I rinsed out my mug and then used the bathroom. When I was finished, I tidied the small space, whistled for the dog, and went down the stairs to start my new job.

CHAPTER 8

WHEN I WALKED across the yard, the two women were sitting silently on the logs by the fire pit, cups of coffee in hand. I noticed that Beverley was looking rather angry. Jess nodded at me and pointed with her mug to where another one stood steaming. As I went to pick it up, Beverley held out her hand in a 'stop' gesture. Her voice was soft but still rather menacing.

"Do not ever," she said, scowling, "call me Bevvy."

Her face opened up and she and Jess both roared with laughter, almost spilling their coffee as they shook with mirth. I shook my head, then took my coffee and sat on one of the spare logs while I waited for them to calm down. After much snorting and wiping of tears, they had both composed themselves.

"Right then," said Beverley. "One thing old Henry said that was right, though. Your hands are too soft, it's obvious you're a city type and not a farmhand. So, we'll need to get that sorted. No work gloves for you, not for the first few days. You need to get some sun and some dirt, some cuts and some callouses. Don't worry, it won't take long."

"We'll finish these and then head down the coulee," said Jess, waving her coffee mug at me. "Did you settle in alright?"

"Yes," I said. "I found the tea bags. Is there a place I can get milk and a few other bits?"

"There's the store in Drumheller," said Jess, "for any major shopping. Or there's a Fas Gas station on the main drag in Hanna, they've got basic stuff like milk."

"And sandwiches," said Beverley. "They do good sandwiches."

"And sandwiches," said Jess, smiling. "But it's basically a convenience store. Nothing too fancy."

"I don't need fancy and if I'm going to be eating with you, then I don't need a major shop. I would just like some milk, maybe some more tea bags, and some snack stuff like almonds or peanuts, things to nibble on if I wake up in the middle of the night and can't sleep. Perhaps a couple of apples or oranges if they happened to have any in."

"I don't think you should go out in public, not yet anyway," said Beverley. "Why don't we look at the set-up down in the coulee, and then while Jess is making dinner, I'll do a run into Hanna and pick you up a few things. You can pay me when I get back. That should tide you over for a couple of days, anyhow, and then you can make a proper list. We usually go into town for a proper shop on Saturday."

"What day is it today?"

"Wednesday. All day!" said Jess, smiling. She put down her mug and stood up. "Come on, let's go."

Beverley and I both drained our coffee, then stood up and followed Jess as she led the way across the yard.

We walked all the way over to the far side of the terrace, some distance from the house, and I suddenly realized that there was a narrow road cutting away down to the right. I paused and looked back, the geography making sense now. The road from the prairie came down to the terrace by the barn and, if it continued straight across in front of the house, would now continue down into the coulee from where we were standing.

"There was a natural terrace here," said Jess, "with a small clapboard house on it. We had that knocked down and then cleared the brush and cut into the back of the hill ourselves, to make the wider space for our house and the barn. So here we are."

She kept walking, dropping down from the terrace and along the gravel road. It was in pretty good condition and easy to walk on. The road went down a hundred metres or so and then switch-backed onto itself a couple of times, lessening the gradient and giving us ever changing views of the landscape. It took about twenty minutes before we were on the valley floor, the base of the coulee. I turned and looked back up the road to the edge of the terrace, which seemed a long way away.

"You'll get used to it," laughed Beverley.

Badger looked at me as if to say, "maybe."

"Come on, this way," said Jess, walking off the road and heading between some scrubby bushes.

"These are sage bush and scrub willow," she said in answer to my unasked question, "and there are larch, spruce and cottonwood down by the river. We'll see those later."

We walked in a single file, with me following Jess and Badger at my heels, then Beverley bringing up the rear. To make sure I don't run away, I thought, smiling to myself. No chance of that, I had absolutely no idea of which way I would need to go. Now that we were off the graded roadbed the ground was soft underfoot, small puffs of dust the result of each step.

The air was still, and I noticed how quiet it was, just the soft brushing of jeans against leaves or the scuff of boots on the ground. As my ears became used to the silence, I realized that there were birds trilling somewhere, a series of musical scales, and that Badger was snuffling against various rocks and plants as we walked.

There was a distinct smell in the air, one I could remember but not quite place, which I then recognized as the scent of the wild sage. A blush of pink revealed itself to be a clump of wild roses, pressed tight against a large grey boulder with a distinctive pink and white pattern threaded through the rock.

"That's an erratic," said Beverley, pointing at the boulder. "It came in the last ice age, from up in the Rockies, carried along by a glacier and dropped here when the ice melted. It's a particular type of quartz that is only found in an area near Jasper, apparently, so that's where it came from. It's nothing like the normal rock around here, which is sandstone, from the time when this was a tropical sea where dinosaurs roamed the shoreline. There's a whole line of these funny coloured rocks scattered across central Alberta, they call it the Foothills Erratic Train apparently, and the scientists can use them to track the movement of the glaciers. Amazing thing, science."

We kept walking, back among the sage bushes now, and then emerged back on to the road. We followed this for another fifty metres and ended up in front of a large barn. It was about twice as wide as the one in which I was staying, but only about two thirds the height, and stood at right angles to the side wall of the coulee.

There was a large door on the end wall, facing out into the coulee, and along the side facing us were two large openings. They reminded me of the bays in a garage, or at the back of a supermarket, the sort of place where a big semi-trailer could be backed in and unloaded. We went to the big end door and I realized that it was on rollers, and Jess slid it open easily.

"We can push the other one as well, so Josef can get his tractor inside," said Jess, as she stepped into a space that was about one third the length of the overall barn. It had a number of large plywood bins constructed against one wall, and a regular sized door at the back. There was a large three pronged fork hanging from two hooks on the wall, and some metal four litre buckets.

"This area is closed off and we keep the hay bales and feed in here," she continued. "That's a pitchfork on the wall, and the feed buckets. Through the door is the open part of the barn, that's for the bullocks, they can go in there for shelter if a big storm comes along. Mostly they just wander around the coulee, though. So, you don't need to worry about them being all inside at night or anything."

"There are just three jobs, really," said Beverley. "First, you check the animals and make sure that they're all here and healthy. No limps or cuts or anything. Second, you'll come through here and then open that back door into the barn proper and take out the hay and feed."

She opened the door and we walked through. On the other side were two troughs, each about ten feet long and two feet wide, and perhaps a foot deep. They were made of some kind of metal, as were the short but sturdy legs on which they rested. A bit further around the barn was a sort of open vase structure, a central circular hub with six metal arms extending upwards at about 30 degrees. Beyond the vase was another trough, this one longer and taking up a good amount of space. It extended out into the barn, but the far end appeared to be tight up against the wall.

"First you bring in five buckets of oats and mixed feed," said Beverley, "and put that in the trough. Make sure it's well spread out along the bottom. It won't seem like a lot but it's a supplement, not the main diet, and we've found that all the animals get enough." She moved on past the troughs, to the vase.

"Then you have to use the big pitchfork to bring in the hay," she said. "Just load it up from the bale out there, then carry it in and dump it in the feeder here." She pointed up at the vase. "It might take you a while to get the hang of it but once you've figured it out, it will be easy. And don't worry if you drop some. We don't have bedding as such, but we do spread a bit of hay around, it makes it easier when we sweep out the manure from the barn."

We kept walking and ended up at the larger trough, which I now realized was for water. There was a tap situated on the wall about four feet from the ground, a length of green hosepipe screwed into the tap. The other end of the pipe was in the trough.

"So, every time you come down here, check the water, and make sure it gets filled up to here." Beverley indicated a dark line scratched into the inside of the trough, about three inches from the lip. "Once a week you need to drain the water, using the sluice end."

She walked to the other side of the trough, the one in the middle of the barn, and showed me that there was a larger length of pipe running from the trough to the outside.

There was a round metal watercock of some sort between the pipe and the trough.

"Just open the valve", said Beverley, "and the water will run out. Empty the tank once a week and then rinse it from the main pipe. Then close up the valve and fill it up again."

"Why do they need clean water?" I said. "I thought cows drank anything."

"Well, they do," said Jess, joining the conversation. "But we've found that freshening the water once a week seems to help. We've certainly not had any problems with them getting sick."

"Also," said Beverley, "you'll remember I was talking about Palliser and the droughts. Well, if you come here, please."

We walked out of the barn, following the line of the outflow pipe as it extended into the sage along the base of the coulee wall. It stopped at a large green metal box, which seemed buried in the ground. A smaller pipe came vertically out of the box and rose up the side of the wall, held on with clamps of some sort and disappearing over the ridge.

"So, this is our reservoir tank," said Beverley. "Here we store the wastewater from the cattle trough, then pump it up to the farm when we need to irrigate the kitchen garden. 'Waste not want not' is our mantra, whenever possible that is."

"That's pretty clever," I said.

"Thank you. We think so as well."

"Does it get sludgy?"

"Good question. Yes, some sediment does build up. Every three years we take the lid off this tank," said Jess, pointing at the green box. "Then we use a bucket and spade combo to take up as much of the mud as we can get out. It's not perfect but it seems to leave enough room for the water which accumulates in between times."

"We do that in the late summer, before the cattle come down," said Beverley, smiling. "And guess what? It's due to be emptied this year, so that's going to be one of your jobs."

I looked at her.

"OK," I said, "but where do I put the stuff, after I've got it out?"

"That old wheelbarrow by the barn," she said. "You put it in there and then take it ..."

"Up there!" I said. "To the garden? Up that road? There's no way ..." I started spluttering, the idea of pushing a wheelbarrow up that hill giving me palpitations.

Jess and Beverley both looked at me and laughed.

"No, don't be silly," said Jess. "You take it over to the other side of the barn, where we have a big compost pile. We keep the barn sweepings there as well. When it has all rotted down a bit then we take it up to the garden, yes, but we use the old truck for that."

"Anyway," said Beverley, "that's about it for here. We'd like you to empty the reservoir tank first, so that's cleaned out before the cattle come down. Josef should be here at the beginning of next week, so you can help him offload the hay bales and stack them inside. Then we'll move the cattle down, you can help us with that, and after that you'll come down every day to feed and water them, and to sweep out the barn. Can you handle that?"

"I think so, sure," I said.

"Great. Well, it's getting a bit late," said Jess, looking at her watch. "It's after six already. I should go and get dinner started."

"We can all walk up," said Beverley. "Tomorrow we'll go for a proper look around the coulee, down to the river and the camp site." She looked me over, critically. "Have you ever ridden a horse?"

"Umm, no," I said.

"Well, that can be tomorrow's adventure," said Jess. "We've got a couple that are good for our greenhorn guests, it will do them all good to have a day out. Right now, though, time for home."

Jess turned and led the way, this time following the road instead of cutting through the brush. I realized that we were curving around more boulders, other remnants of the ice age I assumed, and that there really wasn't that much difference between the road and the path. Soon we began to climb, and at the first switchback I stopped and looked back.

"What a great view," I said, bending forward and resting my hands on my thighs.

"Scenic break?" asked Beverley, laughing. "That's what we call it, when what we really mean is that we need to catch our breaths."

"Whatever," I said. After a few minutes I could stand straight. Beverley and Badger were looking at me, Jess was already up the hill and disappearing around the second bend.

"Come on then," said Beverley. "It will get easier the more often you do it."

Saying that she set off again, and I slowly followed behind. Badger ran back and forth between us, his tail wagging like a short little flag, and although Beverley reduced her pace I still kept falling behind. I took another couple of scenic breaks along the way, and by the time I crested the coulee she was already sitting on the logs and there was a fire blazing in the pit.

The light was starting to fade, I noticed, and the sky up over the prairie had started to redden with the first rays of sunset. The lights were on in the house, and through a window I could see Jess moving backwards and forwards in the kitchen. Beverley handed me a beer.

"Sit a while," she said.

I sat down on a log and faced out from the house, Badger lying down beside me. The far sidewall of the coulee was catching the sun, turning various shades of red and gold beneath the darker eastern sky. I sipped my beer and lazily scratched Badger behind the ears.

"Makes you wonder what the rich people are doing, doesn't it," said Beverley, raising her can. I raised mine and we tapped them together.

"Cheers," we said, in unison, then sat in silence as the colours changed. The fire crackled and had nearly burned down to embers when Jess called from the house.

"Come on in, you two, dinner's ready."

Beverley stood up and took some sandy soil from a bucket next to the fire. She threw it on the embers, then poured the rest of her beer on top. The sand sizzled and smoked.

"Just in case a wind comes up," she said. "Fire can spread pretty quick out here in a wind."

I had been about to guzzle the last inch of my own beer but decided to follow her example. Again, there was a sizzle and a puff of smoke.

"That'll do her," said Beverley, and both Badger and I followed her across the yard and up the steps into the house.

CHAPTER 9

AND THEN BEGAN what was without a doubt one of the most interesting two weeks of my life.

Early the next morning we took the truck up to the prairie, to see the bullocks and the horses. At Beverley's suggestion I left Badger on a line tied to the edge of the barn. I drove the truck back down to the yard while Jess and Beverley rode down, a third horse brought along behind on a line. They dismounted and came over to where I stood near the house. Badger had been glad to see me, he must have thought he was being left behind. I untied him and he sat next to me as I looked at the arrivals.

"Right, this is yours," said Jess, gently pulling the rein and bringing the third horse over to me. It seemed a very large animal, especially when it got close. Beverley brought a saddle over and put it on the horse's back, tying some kind of leather straps under the belly. The horse just stood there while I looked up at it.

"Um, how do I get on it?" I said.

"Like this," said Beverley. A small block was pulled out from under the deck, apparently something for me to stand on as I tried to get up on the saddle. Eventually I managed, although I found it terrifyingly high, and gripped anxiously to the reins.

"Just relax," said Beverley, laughing, "she'll do all the work. As long as you don't fall off then you'll be OK."

That was easier said than done, I thought, trying to remain vertical and yet convinced that with every step I would slide off one side or the other. The horse walked around the yard three or four times, never really lifting its head, just looking at the ground. Bored out of her mind, I thought.

"What's her name?" I said.

"Nancy," said Jess, and the horse stopped, lifted her head, and pricked her ears. "Are you doing OK?"

"I think so. As long as I don't breathe it should be fine."

Jess laughed.

"Just think of all those cowboy movies you watched as a kid," she said. "Remember how they kind of slouched a bit, that's to stop feeling every step. Your body has to become like a shock absorber, so you move with the horse and don't get moved by the horse. Don't worry, we won't be galloping, not even trotting. Just a nice leisurely walk down the road and into the coulee."

She and Beverley walked away and nonchalantly climbed up onto their horses, using the pommel as a sort of lever and the stirrups as a hoist. They came back over to me and I realized their horses were even bigger.

"Right then," said Jess. "Come on, Nancy."

She turned and walked her horse across the yard, Nancy following behind. To my right I could see Badger trotting along, keeping a good distance away but staying within my line of sight. I realized that Beverley had moved into third place behind us, although I did not look back to check. I clenched the pommel and tried to stay as vertical as possible.

When we started down the road from the terrace to the coulee I automatically leaned backwards a little, trying desperately to focus only on Nancy's ears so that I did not have to be reminded how far it was down to the bottom of the valley.

We picked our way down, Nancy following Jess at a distance of about ten feet. It seemed to take a long time but suddenly I realized that we were now walking on a level surface and had made the base of the coulee. I relaxed a little and managed to look around.

The view was different from when we had walked to the barn, now I was higher and could see over the sage and scrub bushes. Small tendrils of dust, scented with the oils released from the leaves we had brushed against, rose up around me. The sun was warm on my neck. Beverley rode up beside me.

"OK," she said. "We made it down. Well done. Now let go of the pommel and hold onto the reins."

I did as she asked, one hand at a time, but soon was sitting there with my elbows by my sides, my arms stretched forward. None of this seemed to make the slightest bit of difference to Nancy, who just kept plodding along at the same pace.

We came round the trail in front of the barn, passed across the yard, and then continued past the dung heap and onto a smaller, narrower trail. This took us in a more or less straight line, with some elongated curves around the larger trees and, once, a semi-circle past some more large erratic rocks. We rode for about half an hour, I suppose, and then I realized we were aiming towards a stand of larger trees.

"See those cottonwoods?" said Jess, over her shoulder. "That's where we're heading."

The trees got larger and in another ten minutes we were approaching their shade. Jess stopped and jumped down from her horse, as did Beverley. Nancy stopped between them and stood there, quietly, while I didn't move.

"Come on, then," said Beverley, "down you come."

I looked at her, and then down to the ground.

"How?"

She laughed.

"OK, first hold on to the pommel again. Then lean forward and start to slide down to your right a bit, lifting your left leg so it clears her back. Once you have both legs on this side, just jump down".

I followed her instructions, freezing a couple of times as I felt myself losing control. At last I dropped to the ground, where I immediately fell over. And sat in the dirt.

"We might need to keep practising that," said Jess.

Badger came over and licked my face.

"Aw, cute," said Beverley.

I scrambled to my feet and looked around. We were in a cleared area that extended past the trees and ended, I saw, at the bank of a river. It was not a particularly wide river, perhaps twenty metres, and I could see more sage brush on the other side.

"We'll tether the horses and then show you the camp," said Jess, passing me a long piece of rope. I watched as she fastened a similar piece to the halter of her horse, using a small calliper type clip, and then tied the other end of the rope to a large log that had been nailed across the top of two posts. I went to do the same, but she stopped me, and gestured over the clearing. I realized that there were a number of the log and post contraptions scattered around.

"Tether one horse to one hitching post," she said, "otherwise if they get startled by something, they might hurt each other."

I couldn't really see Nancy being startled by anything but nonetheless walked across to the next post, clipped the rope to the halter, and then tied the other end to the log. Beverley finished hitching her horse and the three of us moved towards the river. Badger was sniffing at some small plants that lined the bank, underneath a row of large trees which cast shade onto the water, and I saw that the bank on the other side was deeply cut. Beverley saw where I was looking.

"The current sort of swings out over there," she said, "and so it erodes the bank more. That's also where the water is a bit deeper. In close here where we are the current is pretty soft, and you can see how shallow the river is."

I looked down and realized that I could actually see small stones and pebbles on the bottom of the river. Beverley pointed to our right.

"If you want to go for a swim, the best thing is to go in up there, by the third cottonwood. Then once you're in the water, you'll feel the current. Just float on it and it will take you across the river to that bank, where it gets to about six or seven feet deep. So you can dive and splash around in there, then either swim straight back over to here or else float down to the tipi."

I looked to the left and saw a tipi on the edge of the bank, on our side of the river but about a hundred metres away.

"The current comes back over and then follows this side for a while, so it's easy to climb out," said Jess. "You could also go in the water here, and wade up to the cottonwoods, if you don't mind walking on stones."

"This is the trekker camp you use?" I said. "It's pretty perfect."

"Yes, we think so," said Beverley. "Let's get a fire going then go for a swim. Coffee will be ready when we're finished."

"I didn't bring a swim suit," I said.

Beverley just looked at me. Jess was kinder.

"It's OK," she said. "We figured that out. Go up to the tipi and have a look in there, we keep a stock of different sized shorts for people who either didn't bring swimming gear or else decided that what they did bring wasn't appropriate. Fire first, though."

I helped bring over a few armfuls of wood from a pile that had been hidden under an old grey tarpaulin.

"This is another job for you, by the way," said Beverley. "If you have any spare time and fancy a walk and a swim down here, that's OK, but you should always cut some more wood and stack it to dry. We can never have enough, some of the tourists will burn a whole stack on a single bonfire."

Once the fire was going, I went off to the tipi. Ducking inside the air was cool, even though the sun was shining and it was away from the protection of the tree shadows. I saw what looked like an old steamer trunk sitting against one wall, and when I opened the lid, I found the collection of clothes, including jeans, shirts, and shorts.

I rummaged through and found a pair my size, then stripped off my trousers and put on the shorts. I kept my shirt on but left my boots, socks, and pants at the back of the tipi. I went back across the clearing and found that Beverley and Jess had both removed their jeans and riding shirts and were now wearing shorts and t-shirts. A blackened pot sat at the edge of the fire.

We walked away from the fire and into the shade of the

cottonwoods, following a narrow but visible trail that curled to the left at the third large tree and led us to the bank. The earth had been cut and two flat stones lain as steps, one slightly raised from the other, so we could simply walk down and into the river. It was cold, but not too unpleasant. I could feel the push of the current against my ankles and calves.

"Like this," said Beverley, taking two steps further into the river and then suddenly dropping into deeper water. She resurfaced a few feet away and turned onto her back, floating. The current moved her across the river.

Jess followed her, taking two good steps and then disappearing under, popping back up a moment later and also turning to lie on her back, face to the sun, as she drifted slowly after Beverley.

"What the heck," I thought, and took two steps after them. As my foot came down the second time, I realized that there was no riverbed anymore, and I just kept going, plunging underwater with a gasp, my head going in before I had time to close my mouth. I went straight down and then felt stones under my feet. I bent at the knees and pushed against the riverbed, trying to keep my mouth closed as I flailed upwards.

It seemed to take a long time but at last I broke through the surface and spat out river water before gulping lungs full of air. I wiped my eyes with my hand and stared madly around. Beverley and Jess were standing a few feet away from me, waist deep in the river, convulsed with laughter.

On the bank, Badger barked twice, then turned and went back to the camp site.

"We forgot to say," Jess said, "there's a bit of a hole there, if you're not expecting it then it can be a bit of a shock. The rest of the river on this side is quite shallow."

The two of them turned and lowered themselves into the water, then drifted off towards the other bank. I allowed myself to calm down, then turned over onto my back, and followed.

We must have stayed in the water for nearly half an hour, splashing around and laughing. The deeper part of the river along the opposite bank extended for about thirty metres, so it was possible to swim lengths as though one was in a pool.

You had to be careful at the ends, though, as the pebbles rose quite sharply up to the shallows. A couple of times I scraped my stomach on the bottom because I overextended my reach and thought I could get another stroke from the swim. My cursing when this happened caused much merriment.

Eventually it was time to leave the water. We lazed back across the river on the current, then clambered out and came up the bank next to the tipi.

"You can change back into your clothes then come up for coffee," said Jess, and walked off towards the fire.

I looked at Beverley.

"Is there anything specific I should use as a towel?" I said.

"I don't think so. Let me look."

She pushed open the flap of the tipi and went inside. I followed and found her looking at the various pairs of shorts that I had found and then discarded next to the steamer trunk.

"None of this is much good," she said, then pointed

across to the other side. "There, behind the door flap, one of those will do."

I turned and saw a number of old blankets hanging from a nail in one of the poles. They were striped with blue and red bands, fraying a bit at the edges, and half-hidden in the shadows so that I hadn't noticed them before. I walked over and pulled the top one down. It was a bit musty but seemed not to be too dirty.

"Great. Thank you," I said.

Beverley nodded, checked as though to say something, then simply walked past me and left the tipi. I stripped off my shorts and shirt, toweled myself dry with the blanket, and then pulled on my long pants, socks, and boots. My shirt was still soaking wet, so I dug into the trunk again and this time found a large blue flannel shirt. It was a bit big on me, but it felt warm and comfortable.

I left the blanket spread out on the old trunk, thinking it would dry faster that way, then left the tipi. I carried my wet shirt back across the clearing, picking up a short stick as I went.

As I approached the fire, Badger rose from where he'd been lying and came over to say hello, his tail waving like a little flag. I saw that both women had already changed back into their riding clothes and were holding mugs of coffee. Sparks sparkled upwards and I realized that someone had put some fresh wood on the fire.

I stuck the stick in the ground about a metre from the fire and hung my own shirt on it to dry. Then I looked for a mug into which I could pour my coffee. I put the pot back by the fire, which was now burning brightly, then turned to find both women staring at me.

"What?"

"That shirt," said Jess.

"What about it?"

"Where did you find it?"

"It was in the old trunk with the other clothes," I said.

Beverley came over and slowly ran her hand down my arm, from the shoulder to the elbow, a long gentle stroke.

"It was my husband's," she said softly. "I'd forgotten it was in there."

I looked at her, then at Jess, then back to her again.

"Your husband?"

"Yes. He died a few years ago."

She saw me looking at Jess again and recognized my obvious confusion.

"Oh, I had a life before Jess," she said. "A lot of life. But I left it for her, and we moved here, and then some of the old life sort of ebbed into the new one for a while, and then receded away again. Drink your coffee before it gets cold."

She walked back over to Jess and put her arm around her shoulder, Jess folding into her. We all stood there for a few minutes, rather awkwardly I thought. I sipped my coffee, trying to avoid burning my tongue, and watched the flames. At last Jess disentangled herself and gave her mug to Beverley, then walked over to the horses. Beverley came towards me and threw the remnants of coffee onto the fire, which spluttered and sizzled.

"We'll need water to put it out properly," she said. "Could you bring some up please."

It wasn't a question, and I picked up the coffee pot to empty it out first. Beverley nodded.

"And there's a bucket over there," she said, "by the edge of the river."

I turned and saw a silver pail sitting in the grass at the edge of the clearing. When I went over to pick it up, I realized that there was a length of rope tied to the handle.

"It means you don't have to get wet," Beverley called.

I nodded, then threw the bucket into the river. Pulling it back ashore, I first filled the coffee pot, then the bucket again, and carried the water up to the fire. It took me three trips before the wood stopped sizzling each time it was doused, and only then did Beverley reach in with her boot and stir the embers around. The next time I poured water, steam rose but there was no noise.

"That should be good now," said Beverley. "Let's get back up to the house."

We walked over to the horses and I found that Jess had pulled an old tree stump over for me to use as a step. It only took me five tries to get mounted on Nancy, by which time the other two were already walking their horses across the clearing.

It was only when I was proudly up on the saddle that I realized I had not actually untied the rope from the log, and that Nancy was still quite effectively tethered. I looked around but the women were already out of the clearing and into the sage brush. I climbed down, told Badger to stop looking at me in such a critical way, untied the rope and unclipped it from the halter, then got back up on my horse. This time it only took three tries.

I wound the rope into loops and hung it over the pommel, then lifted the reins and gently tugged to the right. To my amazement Nancy immediately turned in that direction and started plodding off after the others. There was still the faint scent of smoke from the last embers of the fire, but that was quickly overtaken by the smell of the sage dust as we left the clearing.

The sun was low in the sky as we walked through the brush, past the barn and the erratic, then up the road to the terrace and the welcome sight of the house. Once we were in the yard, Beverley called back to me.

"Give me the horse and bring the truck up to the top," she said.

I climbed down off Nancy and passed the reins to Beverley. She and Jess rode off up the road towards the prairie. I went up the steps to my room and changed shirts, then came back and left the blue one on one of the chairs near the door to the house.

On the verandah I stood for a moment, looking back out over the coulee. The sun had started to go down and I was in the shadow thrown by the ridge up to the prairie behind me, but across the valley I could see the bright bands of bed rock shimmering. It was a beautiful sight, and one I knew I would remember.

I reached down and scratched Badger's ears, then we walked across the yard. I opened the tail gate of the truck. He jumped up and I closed the gate behind him, then got into the cab and followed the riders up to the paddock.

CHAPTER 10

THE FOLLOWING days settled into more of a routine. Nothing else was said about the shirt, although someone had picked it up before I next went to the house. I ate my breakfast and dinner with Jess and Beverley, and either was given instructions for the days' work or else reported on what I had accomplished.

I didn't wear gloves and, as prophesied, soon my hands were burnt by the sun and nicked with cuts and scrapes. My fingernails were lined with dirt, and each evening after dinner I would usually just collapse on my bed and go straight to sleep.

Most days Badger and I would walk down the road to the barn, picking up any windblown branches we came across and throwing them into the brush. At the barn Badger would find a shady spot and settle down, while I got on with my chores.

At around lunch time I would stop and pull out the sandwich I'd been given and sit on a log or a rock to eat. Then Badger and I would spend twenty or thirty minutes exploring the area around the barn, each time walking a bit further and each time slightly changing the direction in which we went.

Some of our walks took us out to the river camp, and I would dutifully collect various branches and other deadfall to place under the grey tarpaulin. One lunch break I found myself out by the line of erratic rocks. As I poked around, I saw a small pebble, no doubt a chip from a larger boulder. It was beautifully striped, a rich cream line weaving its way through the red stone. I picked it up and put it in my pocket.

I emptied the sludge tank, taking a dozen or more wheelbarrows full of gunk out to the compost pile, and added to it all the old hay I cleared from the barn. I checked the pipes and the various flanges where they connected to the troughs, and basically got the area cleaned up. I tightened valves and connections, oiled things that needed to be oiled, and generally kept myself busy.

In the late afternoon Badger and I would walk back up to the house. I'd have a shower, then sit on the balcony with a cup of tea until it was time to go over to the house for dinner. It was a pleasant enough routine, strenuous to make sure that I slept well every night, and the days passed quickly.

One morning I heard an engine and an old tractor appeared, pulling a trailer on which were piled twenty round bales of hay. Each was wrapped in a protective white plastic wrap, and they were tied down with lengths of thick green rope. A man jumped down from the cab of the tractor and came over to me. He was younger than I had expected, perhaps about my age. He looked pretty athletic, about six inches taller than me and a bit heavier but not at all fat.

"Hello. You must be the Claude I heard about from the lady. You are to help me, yes?" he said. He had a slight accent, but nothing that stopped me understanding what he was saying.

"Yes," I said. "I'm Claude. And you must be Josef."

I held out my hand and he shook it, but at the same time was shaking his head.

"No, I'm not Josef, I am Adam, his son. My dad slipped on a patch of wet grass the other day, the silly bugger has broken his leg. So, I'm having to do the work."

"Sorry to hear that," I said. "Will he be OK?"

"The doctors think so, yes, but they say he will be on crutches for at least a month, until they can take off the cast. So, this is my new life. OK, can you get the doors open, I shall ready the tractor."

He unlocked the hitch and lifted the heavy towing bar up from the dowel, then let it fall to the side. I left him to it and went over to the big doors, which rolled open easily. By the time I had opened the doors to the barn he was back in the tractor and turning it in a wide circle, so he ended up on my side of the trailer. He turned off the engine and climbed down again.

Together we walked to the trailer and started to unfasten the knots which held the tie ropes to the side bars. Once a rope was untied, we threw it over the top of the bales so that it landed on the ground on the far side. When all the ropes were untied, we went round the other side and made sure they were not still stuck to any of the bales. Adam showed me how to roll the rope and store it underneath the trailer, on a narrow flange below where the rope end was tied to the bar on that side.

He went back to the tractor, which I now saw had two spikes sticking out of the front, a bit like a forklift might. Slowly he approached the trailer and lifted the front lift arms to the correct height, then impaled one of the bales on the top row.

The tractor backed away and Adam lowered the arms, then turned and drove in through the open doors to the barn. He carefully placed the bale towards one side of room, making sure that the exit to the door was clear, then reversed out and repeated the process.

It took just over five minutes to unload and stack each bale, so the task took us almost two hours. We then replaced the coils of rope on the bed of the trailer and hitched the tractor back into the towing bar. It was nearly lunchtime by the time we had finished.

Adam went to the cab of his truck and came over with two cans of soda, passing one to me. We drank thirstily, then he pulled out a packet of cigarettes from his shirt pocket and offered one to me.

"No thanks, I don't smoke," I said. "But you go right ahead."

He nodded, flicked his lighter, and inhaled the smoke with obvious pleasure.

"So, what's it like, living here?"

"Well, I'm not really living here," I said. "Just staying here and working for a couple of weeks."

"Then what?"

"Then I head on the road again. I've got an offer of a place over in Saskatchewan, near North Battleford," I said. "They want me there in mid-September, so I figured I'd help out here and get some money together before I head further east."

"Where did you come from?"

"The last place where I worked was at Jess's dad's. I didn't know that at the time, of course. I just worked there, knew her brother Dave but had no idea she existed until after her dad died. Anyway, after her dad passed and then she and Dave decided to sell his farm, she asked me if I could give them a hand here, so I figured why not. What about you? Do you work with your dad?"

"Me? No," he said. "I live in Red Deer, but when he fell, I had to get a leave from my job and come out here to help him. What did you do before you went to Jess's dad's place?"

"Oh, this and that."

I was getting a bit concerned about all his questions, so decided it was time to get back to work.

"Thanks for bringing down the hay," I said, crushing my soda can. "Beverley and Jess will be pleased to have this job finished."

"Yup," he said, stubbing out the cigarette under his boot and then picking up the filter and putting it in his pocket before climbing back into the cab of the tractor. "Here, give that to me, my workplace collects old bottles and cans as a fundraiser. We cash them in at the recycle place and then donate the money to a kid's charity."

I passed him the can and he threw it into the back of his cab, then pulled off his work glove and extended his hand.

"See you around."

We shook hands, then I stepped back and waved as he started the engine, a large plume of blue smoke came from the exhaust.

"I'd better tell Josef to get that fixed!" he said, laughing, and then drove away across the yard and back along the road up to the terrace. Badger and I stood by the doors to the barn and watched him go.

That evening at supper I asked Beverley if she'd heard any news from Calgary. She said that things seemed to have quietened down, that the Alberta government had signed a peace agreement, and that two new pipelines were being built—one for oil and one for water. The paratroopers had all withdrawn to the Canadian base outside Edmonton, with the soldiers from there taken to the artillery base in Wainwright. That had apparently been turned into a big internment camp, with any civilian who caused trouble also ending up there.

"It's getting quite full, apparently", said Jess, looking up from her meal, "and they've been building a camp of some sort in Kananaskis."

"Who's keeping order, if the troops are in barracks?"

"The police, it seems," said Beverley. "The government has authorised the sheriffs to look after things in the country and the city police forces have had new senior commanders appointed. So, everyone has fallen into line. The public seem to have settled as well, at least on the surface. The traffic lights work, the shops are full, people are being hired for the new pipeline construction projects, public transport is running, so it's all good."

"Those who lost family during the invasion can't be too happy," I said.

"You'd think so," said Jess, "but it seems that the trouble only happened in Calgary. It was blamed on overzealous troops who didn't fully understand their orders. Every next of kin received an apology and a hundred thousand dollars per casualty, no tax involved, and anyone who continued to complain just disappeared, most likely to Wainwright. Others in the family, those who hadn't complained, were offered the money instead. They tended to take it."

"Is that the same across the country?"

"Well, across the west anyway. Control of everywhere from Manitoba to the BC border seems to have passed into the hands of those who either can't, or won't, resist. They're calling it Alsama, after the three provinces. Not very original, but cute."

I looked at them both.

"What do you guys think about all this?"

Jess glanced at Beverley, then turned back to me.

"For me, I don't agree, but I understand," she said. "The central government in Ottawa has always seemed to treat the west like its own personal piggy bank. They just keep pulling out resources, but only those they want, and then telling us we can't take out the things we want. So, we can mine for potash, but not for coal. We can drill for oil, but we can't frack, and we can't ship the oil anywhere because we're not allowed to build pipelines. They'd rather bring oil to the New Brunswick refineries by tanker from Saudi than give permission for us to build a pipeline across Quebec. And why? Politics. If the French are going to get upset, we can forget about being heard. Until they want more money in equalization payments, of course."

Beverley smiled as she shook her head.

"Jess can get a bit animated about this," she said. "People around here thought things would change with the Reform Party, and then when that merged with the Conservative Party, they really hoped that their motto, The West Wants In, would become reality. But even with a western Prime Minister, and strong western voices in Cabinet, the political weight of Ontario and Quebec still overpowered everything else. And to be honest, I think Ottawa misjudged the resentment. They thought it was just a few rednecks out in the oil patch but really, this goes deep through all Alberta. And not just us."

"That's right," said Jess. "Alberta has always taken the lead but Saskatchewan has started to complain as well. Manitoba has tried to keep under the radar but that's been changing as well. So, it's no surprise, really, that they're happy to come in with us. I think Alsama is a good step, going forward."

"What about BC?" I said.

"They're lost in their own little fog," said Beverley, laughing. "There are only three major roads across the Rockies, and they've all been blockaded. So, nobody is getting across the mountains."

I found it all quite depressing.

"I think I'll go to my room," I said.

Beverley stood up at the same time as me.

"Did the feed bales get down today?"

"Yes, they're here," I said.

"Good", said Jess, also standing. "Tomorrow we'll bring down the steers and get them settled in for the fall. Good night, Claude."

"Good night."

I left them and went out to the yard. The stars were incredibly bright, but there was no moon. A meteor blazed across the sky over the coulee, and somewhere I could hear an owl, but otherwise all was quiet. Badger came out from under the deck and fell in step beside me. We walked together back to the barn, and up the stairs to our room.

I WOKE EARLY the next morning and sat on my small balcony with a cup of tea, watching the sun slowly rime the far coulee and then edge its way up over the horizon. I finished my drink and then clumped down the stairs and over to the house for breakfast.

"Ready for another ride?" said Beverley, pouring me a cup of coffee. Jess came over from the sink with our plates, each loaded with two eggs, some fried potatoes, three slices of crisped bacon, and a handful of mushrooms. She went back and got her own plate, also bringing over a plate piled high with slices of toast. I lathered on some butter and took a welcome bite.

"Riding where?" I said.

"We're going to bring the steers down, remember," said Jess.

"And this time no truck," said Beverley, grinning at me. "You're riding both ways, uphill and down. This is cowboy time."

"Yee ha," I said, mournfully, and they both laughed.

We ate steadily, commenting on the weather and the forecast for the next few days, then after clearing away our plates went out to the horses. Nancy seemed to recognize me and whinnied softly as I approached. I passed her a piece of carrot I'd taken from the kitchen, and she crunched it noisily.

"You don't need to bribe her," said Jess. "She'll look after you anyway."

I pulled the little block of wood out from under the deck and used it as a stool to climb up on the horse. I was able to do this first time, which made me feel very proud of myself. Beverley noticed and clapped in my direction, so I bowed to her and she laughed. Then we set off in single file, this time going up the road from the terrace to the prairie. We started to walk along the road towards the paddock.

"What if a car comes?" I said.

"Usually, they'll slow down," said Jess, "but if they don't, don't worry. Nancy will look after you."

We walked in single file for a hundred metres or so, and then Jess leaned down to unlatch a gate into the first paddock, which we entered. The cattle were milling around, obviously not happy with the intrusion, but they didn't cause too much trouble. I was interested to note that from horseback the cattle didn't look anywhere near as big and terrifying as they had when I'd used them to cover my passage across the bridge.

"OK," said Beverley, riding up to me so that the three of us were close together. "Here's how this works. We have to get the cows from here along the road and then down to coulee. The dangerous bit is on the blacktop, from here to our road. That's when they could get spooked by a vehicle or something. So I want you to go back to where we came up, and stay there in the middle of the road to stop traffic until we get past you."

"Just stand there? Will cars see me?"

"Yes, there's a good view. And no, you won't be standing, you'll be sitting. On the horse. So you'll be pretty visible. And people will slow down because they won't want to hit you and get a horse through their windscreen. That'd be as bad as hitting a moose."

"OK," I said, although I was not convinced.

It all went as planned, though. I rode back to the place where the road dropped down to the terrace, then halted Nancy and sat there in the middle of the road. Jess herded the cattle out of the gate to where Beverley sat on her horse, acting both as a guard for traffic coming from that side and also as a cattle director.

I could see her waving her hat and hear an indistinct hollering, and it became apparent that the cattle were coming down the road towards me. Once they were a few metres away I started waving my hat and shouting, and the cows stopped to look at me.

Nancy obviously knew what to do. She stepped towards the lead cow and then stopped. It looked at her with suspicion. She took another step and I could see its nostrils flare. A third step and the bullock stepped sideways, away from Nancy.

She moved forward again, and he started edging off the road and towards the trail. She took another step, and he crossed the verge, followed by the others in the herd. By the time Beverley and Jess rode up, all the cattle were slowly making their way down the road towards the terrace.

"Well done," said Beverley. "Are you sure you haven't done this before?"

"That was all down to Nancy," I said. "I just sat here."

"Come on," said Jess, "we need to keep them moving or they'll be in the garden."

Together we walked down the road, past the barn and the house. Jess and Beverley broke their horses into a trot, one of them on each side of the herd as it crossed the clearing. They guided the cattle past the garden and started them down the trail to the coulee. I called for Badger and he came down from the apartment, then we walked out and followed everyone down the hill.

Once we were at the barn, the cattle spread out into the sage and started grazing.

"They'll be fine now," said Jess. "I'll go back up to the house and leave you two to it." She rode away back up the road, while Beverley and I dismounted. She followed me into the barn.

I filled the big water trough, leaving the hose running while I got the buckets of oats and mixed feed from the bins.

Beverley watched carefully but didn't say anything. Once I had the five buckets transferred, I turned off the hose then went and got the pitchfork. Beverley came into the back room with me.

"Pick the closest bale," she said, "and just slash the wrap so you can get at the hay."

I looked around for a knife or some shears but couldn't see any. She sighed and pulled a hunting knife from under her jacket.

"Like this," she said, and in one quick movement separated the plastic into two halves. She threw one half over the top of the bale and then watched as I took pitchfork after pitchfork into the other room and filled the large metal feed cup. It was scratchy and dusty work but didn't take me too long to finish.

"What about the cattle?" I said.

"What about them?"

"Do we have to show them where the food is?"

"Good question," said Beverley. "And yes, we do. But not for an hour or so. It's their first time in the coulee so we let them get used to this area first, then bring them into the barn. That way when they leave the barn, they'll have some idea as to where they are."

"Do you have to fence the road or anything?"

"No, they tend to stay down here. Once we had a herd that came up in the night, Jess found them in the garden in the morning and she wasn't very happy. But usually they stay down here until we drive them back up in the spring, or they go to market, whichever comes first."

"So, what do we do now?" I said.

"Get your horse and let's go for a swim," said Beverley.

CHAPTER 11

We rode down through the sage to the river and hitched our horses to the log beams. Badger explored excitedly as we gathered firewood and laid a fire, although Beverley wouldn't let me light it.

"No, never leave a fire unattended," she said, obviously forgetting that last time we had lit the fire before our swim. Then she clarified things.

"Jess doesn't care as much, she grew up here and is used to it I guess, but I get quite paranoid about starting a grass fire."

Once everything was done to her satisfaction, we walked up through the cottonwoods to the channel. At the bank she took of her shirt, jeans, and boots, then looked at me.

"The rule is, knickers stay on," she said, then unclasped her bra and stepped out into the river, dipping under quickly and surfacing with a whoop before turning lazily onto her back and floating off on the current.

I followed suit, stripping down to my underwear, leaving my clothes and boots in an untidy pile and wading out into the water. It felt cold after the warm afternoon air, and I also gasped as I surfaced from my initial dunk. I floated across the river after Beverley.

We swam up and down for a while, then Beverley trod water for a few moments.

"Let's go and light the fire and have a coffee before we finish those cattle," she said, and dived under again. I followed her and we clambered ashore by the tipi. She ducked under the flap but soon returned, this time carrying two of the old striped blankets, one of which she draped around her shoulders and the other which she threw at me.

We walked back across to the clearing and I lit the fire while she filled the coffee pot, then stood it to one side of the flames. We sat on adjacent logs, and Badger lay on the ground to my left. The fire crackled and it was not long before we could see and hear the coffee start to bubble, the glass bulb on the lid filling and then emptying in a rhythmic pattern. Beverley reached forward and picked up the pot, so I passed over the cups for her to fill. We sat quietly, then she cradled her cup in both hands, cleared her throat, and looked over at me.

"So," she said. "Here we are."

I wasn't quite sure what to say, so I just nodded.

"I suppose you've been wondering about that old blue shirt," she said. "So, let me tell you what happened."

I hadn't really been thinking about the shirt at all, although I had wondered why Jess had seemed upset when they were talking about Beverley's husband, or possibly ex-husband, but I nodded anyway. Encouragingly, I hoped. I've always liked a good story.

"As I told you, I used to be married. I had a pretty good life, back east. Then one day we had a fire alarm at work, and they sent us home early. I came home and found one of my best friends leaning over the arm of the couch in our living room. My side of the couch. Rutting my husband. Doggy style, as they say. She was still dressed but her skirt was pulled up over her back. Her knickers were on the floor and his pants were down round his ankles. Pale blue, they were. Her knickers. Funny what you remember. They were both enjoying themselves so much that they hadn't heard me come in. I watched and listened for a bit, then picked up a glass ashtray we had and smacked Bill on the back of the head. He just collapsed straight over her back, I must have knocked him out. To be honest, I thought I'd killed him. She kept moaning for a while and then, when she realised that he wasn't pushing back, she opened her eyes. And saw me.

"'You're supposed to be at work,' she said, trying to look over her shoulder at the same time.

"'Don't move, I said. 'How long have you been doing him?'

"She'd had the grace to redden a little.

"'Three months,' she said, looking at the ashtray which I was still holding. 'What have you done?'

"'He's either unconscious or dead,' I said. 'If he's dead then you can explain it to your husband. If he's alive then tell him I've left.

"And I just walked out of there. I didn't take any clothes. I stopped at a bank and withdrew as much money as I could, then went to a mall and bought a whole new outfit. I left the old clothes sitting on the bench in the dressing room. Same with shoes, boots, even a suitcase in which to put everything. My credit card got a good workout, that's for sure, but I didn't care, it was in Bill's name and he got the bills. Then I went to the airport and bought a business class ticket on the next flight to Toronto.

"That was leaving in three hours, so I checked in and

went through security, then up to the little business class lounge they had. I had three or four gin and tonics before they called my flight. On the plane I thought about joining the mile-high club but there was nobody I fancied enough to drag into one of those little toilets, so I had another couple of drinks and then a snooze. In Toronto I got my bag and checked into that hotel that's actually at the airport, the one where you have to get the little train that goes between terminals. I slept for a couple of hours then got up, had a shower, put on some of my new clothes, and went down to the bar. It's a pretty dark place, all wood panelling, but it didn't take long for someone to see me.

"He was on his way to a conference, apparently, and had to lay-over in Toronto then catch an early flight the next day. He bought me a couple of drinks and we chatted, he showed me some wallet photographs he had of his kids, then I invited him up to my room to look at the view from the top floor. Which wasn't really fair, as he spent most of the next few hours either looking down at the pillow while he did me missionary style or up at the ceiling while I rode him like a cowgirl. He didn't seem to mind the subterfuge, though. He did get see the view when I leaned up against the window, breasts pressed against the glass, and he took me from behind. I wanted to see what my friend had found so enthralling. To be honest, it didn't do much for me. Around midnight I told him to give my love to his wife and threw him out, had another shower, and then slept through until late the next morning.

"I went into Toronto on the Pearson Shuttle and found myself right downtown, so I wandered until I found an apartment place which had a spare unit to rent. It took a couple of weeks but soon I had moved my bank account and everything to Ontario, and I put my past life behind me. I heard from a friend, not the one who'd been sprawled over my couch but another one, that Bill was OK although he'd had headaches for a couple of weeks. Apparently, he was telling everyone I'd had a bit of a breakdown and walked out. Eventually I e-mailed him and told him that I was taking my share of our bank account plus half of his share, and that I as far as I was concerned, we were now divorced. He could do what or who he wanted, and I didn't expect to see him again. Then I changed my e-mail address and bought a new phone."

Beverley stopped talking for a moment and held out her cup. I silently refilled it. Then she continued.

"I had good office experience and it didn't take me long to get a job as a temp, then after a couple of months this place where I used to go every couple of weeks offered me a full-time job. So, I took that, and did well, and after a while got promoted to an even better job. I upgraded my apartment to a small bedsitter place on the edge of Chinatown and basically was enjoying life in the city, taking the streetcar to work, working hard, and going out for a drink with friends from the office on Friday evening. On weekends I went to galleries, especially the AGO, and sometimes on Saturday evening I'd go to a comedy club or a film or whatever. I dated a few guys and went home a couple of times with some of those, but nothing serious.

"Then one Saturday I was in the Henry Moore gallery at the AGO, daydreaming, running my hand over the flank of one of those big reclining nude sculptures that are there. This voice said, 'I'd like it if someone touched me like that.' I jerked around and there was this blonde woman, a couple of years younger than me, standing there watching me. The rest of the gallery was empty.

"I remember she was wearing a sundress, pale yellow,

and the light in that gallery is weird, it shines in from odd directions. I could see the outline of legs. Funny that I noticed that.

"'I'm sure you wouldn't have any trouble finding someone to do that,' I said.

"She sighed, then said, 'oh, you'd be surprised,' and started to cry.

"I said 'whoa', or something equally inane, and she turned around and literally ran out of the gallery. I just stood there. Then a group of younger kids came in and started hooting around, some adults trying to hush them, so I left and walked down the outside corridor to the little coffee shop they have there. I got an espresso and sat looking out at the street, at the cars and streams of pedestrians, and at the row of galleries in the houses on the other side. Then I felt a hand on my shoulder and the voice said, 'can I explain?'

"I didn't trust myself to speak so I nodded, and the blonde, who you will have guessed was Jess, came and sat opposite me. She had a latte of some sort, one of those designer ones, low fat extra foam soy milk or whatever. She told me that she had just broken up with her partner and was feeling really low and depressed, but she thought I'd looked so caring and sensitive, and she didn't know why but it had just made her cry.

"I laughed and told her I was lots of things but likely not caring and sensitive, I'd left my partner by smacking him on the head with a heavy glass ashtray. She giggled at that, and we started to chat, and that's when I found out her ex-partner was another woman. I'd never really spoken with a gay person before, at least not about their love life, and so it was all a bit strange. We left the gallery and walked down Dundas, she laughed when we came to the first cross street.

"'Look, it's called Beverley Street,' she said. 'Let's go this way'.

"We walked down and at the far end saw a sign to the Rooftop Bar of the Beverley Hotel, so we went up. It was still early, and we were lucky enough to find a spare table. We ordered drinks and some food, tacos I recall, and kept talking, it seemed like for hours, until the lights strung on wires across the open patio came on. Suddenly I realized how late it was.

"'I'd better get off home,' I said, 'where are you going?'

"She just looked at me.

"'I'll try and get a room here,' she said. 'It seems like a nice place.'

"'You mean you don't have an apartment?'

"'No. It wasn't mine it was hers. I'm actually on the street.' She gave a short bark of nervous laughter.

"'Well, that's crazy,' I said. 'I've got a big couch. You can stay on that tonight and tomorrow do what I did when I first got here, look in the paper for rentals.'

"We walked up along to Spadina and then north, towards Chinatown. Suddenly Jess grabbed my arm and pulled me onto a streetcar, dropping two tokens into the machine and grabbing the transfers. When I protested, she just said 'humour me'. We went past my apartment but I didn't say anything, and things became clearer a few stops later, when we got off the street car and she ducked into the LCBO store. I waited and she emerged with two bottles of wine.

"'I didn't know if you liked red or white,' she said. We crossed the road and took the next streetcar south, then got off at Sullivan and walked into Chinatown, to my small apartment. It was on the third floor of an old brick building, no elevator, and both the entry hall and the stairs looked dark and grimy. I opened the door.

"'It's not much but it's home,' I said. She walked in and put the wine on the table. I mentally patted myself on the back for having cleaned up that morning. There was a small sink and stove to one side, with the door to the bathroom crammed up against the fridge.

"'The washroom is through there,' I said, 'but it's a bit of a squeeze to get in. There is a bath, though.'

"'It looks lovely,' she said. 'Now, where's the corkscrew?'

"And so, things progressed as you might imagine. We drank wine, and talked, and drank more wine, and then it was bedtime, so I made up the couch in the living room. Once we were organized, I left her to it, and went to bed."

Beverley looked at me, holding out her cup again. I refilled it, then realized the pot was empty so I placed it on the grass.

"There still seems to be a bit of a gap between you two hooking up in Toronto and then living here," I said. "And where does your husband come back into the story?"

"Are you cold?" she said. "I am."

We stood up at the same time, awkwardly, and then did that silly dance that you do when you're trying to keep out of each others' way, but you actually end up bumping into each other. She clutched me by the shoulders, falling into me, and I felt her breasts press into my chest, her nipples erect and hard.

"I told you I was cold," she said, then turned her face up and kissed me. "Remember the rule."

It wasn't that difficult to keep to the rule, as it turned out. Beverley threw her blanket to the ground and sank down on it, holding me tight and pulling me with her. I caressed her and kissed her, then walked my hand down across her stomach to find the warmth between her legs, and I was able to simply pull the gusset aside before I entered her. It was quick and animal like, pure lust rather than anything else, and we were both panting heavily when we finished. I rolled onto my back and lay next to her.

"Knickers still on," I said with a laugh, once I had my breath back.

She stroked the back of my hand with her thumb.

"Thank goodness for Y-fronts," she said, "and the stretching effect of waterlogging. Do you mind if I smoke?"

"No, of course not. I didn't know that was one of your vices."

"Other than screwing the help, you mean? No, I don't smoke a lot, usually just a couple a day."

She got up and went over to her clothes, pulling on her shirt and taking a crumpled pack of cigarettes from the breast pocket. She leaned toward the fire and took out a small fiery branch, holding it to the end of her smoke and inhaling with a sigh of pleasure. Then she sat down next to me again.

"So, go on, what happened after you took Jess into your bed?" I said.

Beverley looked at me in astonishment.

"No, that's not what happened. She seduced me, not the other way around. Jess knew what she wanted, and she went out and got it."

It was my turn to be astonished.

"But I thought you were the dominant one, I guess I'd call it the husband, in this relationship", I said.

"Oh no. I'm Jess's wife, and pleased to be that lucky person," she said. "Let me tell you the rest of the story.

"So, I was in my bed and Jess was on the couch, then at about three in the morning I went to the bathroom. When I came out and got back into bed, Jess was already in there, just waiting for me. She asked me if I was OK with this and I said I wasn't sure, then she told me to relax and started to kiss me and tickle me with her fingers. And pretty soon I was lost, in the moment, in her, in everything. And in the morning, she moved in.

"We were together for about three months in Toronto and then one day she got a call that her mom was not well. She flew back to Alberta immediately, and after about a week called to say things weren't looking too good and could I take some time off work to go out and support her. Which I could, and did, and so I got to meet her mom and dad, and her brother. We stayed for a couple of weeks but her mom seemed to rally, so then we came back to Toronto.

"A few weeks later her mom passed, so we went back again, and then some time after the funeral we were surprised to find that she had named Jess and her brother as beneficiaries to a big life insurance plan she had. We'd had no idea. Jess started worrying about her dad being out on his own, because Dave was trying to make a life off the farm. It wasn't long after that when we heard this place was for sale, and with the inheritance money plus our savings we had enough to buy the ranch. So, we came out and got legally married, and slowly over the years we've added on, investing in new things as we go.

"We'd been here almost five years when Bill turned up. There was no warning. He just drove down onto the terrace and climbed out of this big SUV, a rental it turned out. He said he'd kept track of me through various friends, and as he was spending a week in Calgary for work, he thought he'd just come out to apologise and to see how I was doing. We had coffee and chatted, and Jess was very polite and suggested he stay the night, in the spare room.

"After supper I asked if he'd like to see the coulee and we walked down here. It was summer, and light until late. We came down and went for a swim, just like we did today, and then we were sitting right here when he said, 'I can see that you're begging for it,' and he raped me."

"Right here?"

"Yes. Then he said nothing ever changes, I always was a slutty little wife, and we went back up to the house. He went into the spare room. I went and had a long shower and when I came out, Jess asked what had happened. So, I told her. She took me to bed and was incredibly passionate, it was almost as though she had been turned on by my story.

"The next morning, she was all sweetness and light with Bill, touching his arm as she served him toast, playing with her hair, laughing at all his silly jokes. She was wearing a dress with a very short skirt, I realized, and it was very tight across her chest. She had also not put on her bra. Even I could see that she was making a play at him.

"'Did Beverley show you the tipi?' she said. When he answered no, she said 'Oh, but you must see it before you go, come on, I'll drive you down for a quick look.' She grabbed the truck keys and went outside and down the steps. He didn't even look at me, he just jumped up and almost ran out of the door after her. He was wearing his office clothes, black dress pants and a light blue long-sleeved shirt. That was the last time I saw him.

"Jess came back about an hour later. She took off her dress and threw it onto the firepit, shook some kerosene over it, and lit it. Then she went inside and had a shower. When she came out, she was wearing her jeans and plaid shirt. I had made coffee and so we sat on the deck.

"'Well, that was easy,' she said. 'He couldn't see anything beyond my tits'.

"'Well, they are rather nice', I said, and she laughed.

"'We got to the clearing and I walked him over to the tipi. When we got there, he started fondling me and feeling me up. I told him it would be easier if we got undressed. He was out of his shirt and pants in seconds and was taking off his underwear when he realized I hadn't moved'.

"'What about you, darling?' he said, standing on one foot and pulling his jockey shorts off the other one.

"'I'm just fine', I said, and pulled out my bush22. He kind of hopped a bit and was about to say something when I shot him."

"What's a bush22?" I asked Beverley.

"It's a 22 rifle, used for shooting gophers and stuff, but you cut down the barrel and you can carry it in your pack. It's not got a lot of range, but it can stop most things, even a bear if you get the eye. It's just a good thing to have in the bush. And we carry one in the truck."

"'So anyway,' said Jess, 'he fell over and I checked he was dead, then shot him again just to make sure. Then I dug a hole in the middle of the tipi and buried him, and then I put that old trunk over the top of the hole, so nobody will see where I was digging. So now he's gone, and you don't have to worry about him again. He should never have taken his knickers off.'

"I asked her what we were going to do about his vehicle, but she had it all figured out. That morning we went to Edmonton in his SUV and left it in the long-term parking lot at the airport. Then we got a shuttle into the city and the country bus back to Hanna. We bought some bits for the truck's engine from the hardware store and grabbed a cab back here. We were back before dark, so we took a bottle of wine and went down to the river. We drank the wine, then went into the tipi and made love, she was so strong with her passion that she made me scream, and we spent the night there. There were no bad dreams, so we figured we had done the right thing."

"Do you intend to tell Jess about us?" I said.

"Probably," she said. "But not until tonight, when we're in bed."

I sat quietly for a moment, picking at the ground under my outstretched hand. I pulled up a handful of debris, small leaves and pebbles, and let them run through my fingers.

"When it's hard to unravel, the grass from the gravel ..." I said, softly.

"I think it's time to be moving to the north country," said Beverley, finishing the lyric.

I stared at her.

"How on earth do you know that?"

"I told you, I had a life before. Down east. Gene MacLellan didn't just make Anne Murray famous, you know. It's not all 'Put your hand in the hand' or 'Snowbird'. Have you heard Gene's daughter sing? Catherine? She's one of those amazing talents, hidden away on Prince Edward Island. Anywhere else in the world she'd be a superstar. Amazing voice."

I just shook my head.

"Well, anyway, yes, I think I might get on the road tomorrow."

"That's probably a good idea. And maybe I won't tell Jess about this until tomorrow night, then I won't have to worry about you hearing me when I scream."

She got up again, threw her cigarette end into the fire,

and walked over to get her clothes. I poured the dregs of the coffee onto the embers, then hauled a couple of buckets of water and made sure there were no red ashes left. Then I went and got dressed as well, and we rode back up to the barn. We showed the cattle where the trough of oats was located, basically by herding them into the barn until one of them started eating and the others followed suit, then rode back up to the house.

"Did you have a good day?" said Jess, standing on the porch.

"Not too bad," said Beverley, "Claude has decided on his plans. He'll tell us at dinner."

We hitched the horses, and she went into the house. Badger and I went up the stairs to our room.

CHAPTER 12

I SHOWERED AND CHANGED, then packed my bag before heading back to the house. Beverley was still in the shower, but Jess was in the kitchen, making supper.

"I went to the bank earlier," she said. "Here's your pay for the past two weeks."

She left the counter and went to her purse, which was sitting on a side table, and came back with a handful of bills.

"There should be twelve hundred there," she said, "as we agreed. But count it, please, just to double check."

I did, and she was correct. I put the money in my back pocket. "Thank you," I said. "I'll take this back to my room."

When I returned, Jess asked me to make drinks, so I mixed up the black rum and ginger beer concoction we'd had at her dad's place. Beverley came down and wrinkled her nose.

"Those things are ghastly," she said, "they make me sneeze."

"It's the ginger," said Jess and I, together, and we all laughed. Jess said that the meal needed to simmer for another twenty minutes, so we went out and sat on the deck. I raised my glass to the coulee.

"These are in honour of my meeting you both," I said. "I'd never had a dark and stormy until I had one with Jess and Dave, so I thought it was a good drink to have to say farewell."

"Farewell?" said Jess.

"Yes, that's the plan that Beverley was talking about. I'm going to head out in the morning, it's time to continue my journey. I'm heading north, up to the river."

They looked at each other, and Beverley shrugged.

"I guess it's time," she said.

"OK, I guess," said Jess. "How are you planning to travel?"

"I thought I'd see if one of you could drop me into Hanna, to that gas station you talk about, and I can ask around when the big rigs stop in, to see if I can catch a ride. If not, then we'll just walk."

"We?"

"Me and Badger," I said, leaning down and ruffling his ears. "I'm not leaving him, I hope."

"No, that's OK," laughed Jess. "Dave said he was yours so that's OK with me. You will enjoy having some company on the road, I think."

She got up and went to the kitchen, then back to the table and served the food. I refilled our drinks and almost overspilled them, they were so full.

"Sorry," I said, laughing as I carried them to the table. "I was trying to finish the ginger beer and the froth seemed to jump up on me."

We had a nice supper, a home-made chili of beans with minced beef, onions, and spices, mopped up with some bread Jess had made that afternoon. We finished the rum drinks then switched to beer, which went well with the chili.

"How was Josef, by the way?" asked Jess. "Was he his normal grumpy self?"

"No, he didn't come," I said. "He's broken his leg or something. His son, Adam, came back from the city to help out. He brought down the bales."

"I didn't know he had a son," said Beverley.

"Yeah, he left home before we moved here," said Jess. "I've never actually met him, but Josef told me about him. He's pretty uninterested in farming, apparently, and after university just stayed away. He's in Airdrie or somewhere, a medic or a firefighter, one of those macho things."

"Lots of kids round here do that," said Beverley. "It's going to be a proper empty quarter if things don't pick up."

"I'll go and see Josef tomorrow," said Jess. "I didn't know he'd broken his leg. Silly fellow, it could have waited. Anyway, I've been thinking."

She stopped eating, holding her fork vertically in the air, then pointing it across the table at me.

"Hitchhiking from Hanna is not a good idea," she said. "You'll be way too obvious. Take the truck."

"What?" I just looked at her, and then across to Beverley, who was nodding.

"Take the truck," said Jess. "It's pretty near full of gas, you should be able to get at least five hundred klicks on it. That'll get you to the river and beyond. When you run out of gas, just leave it. We'll go into town tomorrow and come back in the evening, and then report it stolen the next day. We'll say we thought you'd left it down by the bottom barn."

"That's a good idea," said Beverley. "That will give you a day's start if anyone is looking for you. You'll be well away from here by the day after tomorrow."

"And what do I do with the truck?" I said.

"Just leave it somewhere," said Jess. "It's insured. If someone finds it and we get it back, fine, and if we don't then we'll get the insurance money."

So that was the plan, except for one change. I got back to the apartment after dinner and was sitting on my little verandah, watching the stars. I realized that I'd already said as much of a goodbye as I needed to say. Both Jess and Beverley had been good to me, but it was now time to go. I waited until the lights went out from the house, then Badger and I went down the stairs and across the yard to the truck.

"Come on," I said, and he jumped up onto the passenger seat. I started the engine and drove slowly up the hill to the prairie.

THE DRIVE WAS UNEVENTFUL. I went through Hanna just after midnight, even the gas station was closed, and just drove straight out along the highway to Saskatchewan. I crossed the border at the appropriately named hamlet of Alsask, and then at Kindersley turned north on a minor road.

I still wasn't sure what was happening in the larger centres and I wanted to avoid Saskatoon, so I followed the twenty-one, heading straight north. Well, nearly straight, for there was the weird series of sharp bends around Muddy Lake. I couldn't figure out why they hadn't just built the road a few hundred metres to one side or the other, to keep it straight.

When the road ended at a tee-junction, I turned right. I passed the sign for the World's Largest Tomahawk, at Cut

Knife, but didn't stop, and a short time later I crossed the North Saskatchewan River at North Battleford.

There was a police cruiser parked in the shadow of the gas station on the long climb up from the bridge, but nobody came out after me as I drove past. I drove through the rolling hills and soon saw the glow of the lights from Prince Albert competing against the dawn on the eastern horizon. The 'please refill gas soon' light came on just after six in the morning, as I came over the bridge and into the downtown area.

The first place I saw was a Humpty's Restaurant, so I pulled in there. It didn't open until seven, so I took Badger and we walked back across the road and on to the Rotary Trail, which snaked along the riverbank. It was a lovely fresh morning and it felt good to get the kinks out after such a long drive.

The grass was still green here, lovely to see after the brown of Alberta, and a group of pelicans floated stately by, pushed eastward by the current. There didn't seem to be anyone around, so I let Badger off-leash and he ran madly around, sniffing at all the strange scents, every so often running back to check in with me before taking off into a different set of bushes.

When I smelled smoke, I called Badger back and put him on the leash again. I walked a bit further and saw a flash of blue in between the trees, which after another few yards I realized was a tent. The spiral of smoke was coming from a campfire just at the edge of the clearing. I turned around and walked back towards the restaurant.

Before we left the bank, I took Badger to the water's edge and made sure he had a long drink, then we returned to the truck. I lifted him inside and cracked open the window, then locked the vehicle and walked over to the restaurant, which had just opened. I wasn't the first person through the doors, however, and it was a few minutes before I could order the 'Famous Cowboy Breakfast', with extra sausages and bacon, and a bottomless cup of coffee.

The coffee was fresh and hot, and when the food came, I realized how hungry I was. I wasn't sure how good my will power would be, so I wrapped the extra sausage and bacon in a paper napkin and put it in my pocket, before I was tempted to eat that as well.

Then I took my time, enjoying the food and the coffee and watching the other diners as they visited with each other. It was obviously a popular meeting place, and people yelled 'usual please' to the waitress as they came in and crossed over to wherever their friends were seated. It was only after my third coffee that I realized some were starting to look at me, perhaps not wondering who I was but certainly recognizing that I was a new face, not normally part of their routine.

I got up and paid, then used the restroom. On the way back I bought two coffees to go, one black and the other with a double cream and two sugars. I thought about taking Badger with me and decided against it. It wasn't too hot, and as long as the window was open, he would have enough air. I went to the truck and fed him the bacon and sausage, much to his delight, and then relocked the cab before walking back to the river.

This time I made some noise, purposefully stepping on some dry leaves and coughing as I walked. As I approached the tent, a man stood up from the chair next to the fire. He was tall, well over six feet, with long dark hair loosely tied in a ponytail. His red and black lumberjack jacket was open, and I could see the knife sheath on his belt. I stopped a few yards away and nodded at him.

"Good morning."

He nodded back.

"I wondered how you'd take your coffee," I said, holding out my hands with the two cups.

"Cream and two sugar," he said, then laughed when I stepped forward with the cup in my right hand.

"Is the other one black?" he said. "That's what I'd have done."

I nodded again and waited until he gestured me to join him. There was only the one chair by the fire, but there was an old stump across from it, so I sat there. I raised my paper cup to him, and he returned the gesture. We sipped the coffee in silence.

Eventually he looked up from the fire.

"You're not from PA," he said.

"Nope," I said, then looked at the fire again. We sat quietly for a few more minutes.

"So, how can I help you?" he said, looking up at me.

"I'm looking for someone who might be willing to make a trade," I said.

"A trade of what, for what?"

"A trade of a canoe, for a truck," I said.

"Now who would want a rusty old Dodge Ram?" he said.

I looked at him in surprise, but he just smiled.

"I followed you back, the first time you came here. Earlier, with the dog. What, you thought you'd crept up on me without me noticing? Ha! How was your breakfast?"

"It was fine, thank you," I said.

"Good. Now what sort of canoe are you looking for?"

"Just one that's big enough for me and my bag, and the dog, to go down the river a ways. But not too big, I'm on my own and have not spent much time on the water recently."

"Have you asked your dog how much time he's spent on the river?"

"No, I just thought ..." I mumbled to a halt, realizing that I hadn't really thought this one through properly.

"Go and find a hotel, get some sleep, and then tomorrow morning be at the Funky Fresh at nine thirty. I'll meet you there and you can buy me coffee and breakfast. It's better than Humpty's."

"Where is it?"

"If you're going to navigate the river, you'd better be able to navigate PA," he said, and then stood up and went into his tent. I took my coffee cup and walked back along the river to the parking lot.

I FOUND A GAS STATION, first, and put twenty dollars worth of fuel in the truck. I managed to pick up a road map of Saskatchewan and Manitoba, which had the advantage of showing the river, but it was not very detailed.

I asked advice about accommodations, and it didn't take long to find a hotel with vacancies, one which would allow me to pay in cash and which would accept dogs 'as long as they were well behaved', but they wouldn't let me check-in until noon, so I put Badger back on leash and we wandered the streets of Prince Albert. I found a couple of coffee shops which still had outdoor tables set up and sat at each of them for an hour while Badger lay at my feet. In both cases I soon found young women stopping to say hello and ask if they could pet him, so we both found the waiting worthwhile.

At the first table, one lady came by twice, the second time sitting down opposite me while she had a cigarette and sipped her latte. She scratched Badger's ears and asked me a few questions about myself, and then told me she was also new to Prince Albert and looking for a place to crash. I thought about inviting her back to the hotel but decided against that, for one thing she looked a lot younger than me and secondly, she had the twitchy awareness of a drug user, constantly tapping her leg and flicking her eyes from side to side.

I finished my coffee and told her I'd let her know if I heard of any places where she might stay. She looked disappointed, but gave me her name and phone number anyway, writing her information in a childish block-print on a napkin that had come folded up by her cup. I took the paper and put it in my pocket, then stood up and walked away. Badger looked back a couple of times, but I didn't.

I went back to the river and walked around there for a while, then asked a passer-by where I might find the Funky Fresh Café. Following the directions, I came to a small cheery café, with a chocolatier next door. The café was doing a brisk trade in early lunch sandwiches, it seemed, and so I continued on my way and returned to the hotel. They let me check in, even though it was not quite noon, and I found our room on the third floor. Badger lay down on the floor by the bed while I had a long hot shower, and then I slept.

When I awoke it was after five, and Badger was curled up on the bed, by my feet. He rolled over when I got up but then went back to sleep. I made coffee with the materials provided, and the last drips were spluttering through when I came back from using the bathroom and getting dressed. I turned on the television and watched the local news while I had my coffee, then took Badger and went down the stairs to the street.

A mid-September evening in northern Saskatchewan

gets cool pretty quickly, and I was glad to be wearing both a coat and a hat. Badger and I walked around for a while, and when he did his business, I picked up using a plastic bag I found in my pocket. After a couple of circuits of the downtown core it was getting late, so I went back to the hotel and ordered room service, with a couple of beers for me and an extra burger for Badger. I watched some rubbish on television while I ate, and then pulled the napkin out of my pocket.

What was Rosemary doing, I wondered. Had she found a place to sleep for the night? What would she trade for a night in a warm bed? I considered the options for a while, and then decided I didn't really want the hassle, so I put the napkin into the side pocket of my pack and went to bed.

The bedside phone rang at seven thirty to let me know this was my wake-up call, but I was already up. In fact, I'd already been outside, taking Badger for a morning constitutional just after dawn. I'd been able to walk down the stairs and out through a back door directly into the car park, and back in the same way, so I hadn't had to argue again with the desk clerk as to whether or not Badger was a well-behaved dog.

He'd phoned me in the middle of the night to say that some other guest had complained about Badger howling, but I'd just pointed out that he was a hound dog and must have been having a bad dream. After Badger and I got back from our early walk I had another shower and packed my bag, then about an hour later went down and out through the lobby, dropping my key at the desk as I went.

There had only appeared to be street parking near the café and so I left Badger in the truck at the hotel while I walked down to the liquor store and then turned left on ninth. The cross-grid layout of prairie towns makes them easy to navigate. As my hotel was on First Avenue East, at the junction with Thirteenth Street, and the café was in the eight hundred block of Central Avenue, I basically had to walk five blocks down and one across. I passed a small grocery store and went inside, buying some nuts, some dried fruit, and a couple of sandwiches, all of which I put in my pack.

I got to the Funky Fresh at nine twenty-five. I sat at an empty table by the window and told the waitress that a friend was joining me, and a minute later he walked in. To my surprise he seemed well known here, both the customers and the staff nodding at him respectfully. He came over and sat down across from me. The young raven-haired lady behind the counter wiped her hands and came over to greet him.

"Tansi, uncle," she said, "would you like your usual breakfast?"

"Mananto. Yes, please," he said, "and the same for my friend here. He likes his coffee black, though. Oh, and only one bill, he's paying."

"Of course," she said, then nodded at me, looking at my arm.

"That's a bad scratch on your wrist," she said. "Would you like a Band Aid?"

"It should be OK," I said. "That's what happens when you try to take a treat from a dog." I laughed. "I put some polysporrin on earlier, I'll just let it dry out now."

"As you like," she said, and went back behind the counter.

The man looked at me steadily.

"Did you sleep well?"

"Yes, thank you," I said. "It was a nice hotel."

"It's changed over the years," he said. "It used to be the best hotel, at least for those of us from the north."

"This is the north," I said, remembering the cool evening from yesterday.

"Pah! This is central at best. The north is a long way from here. Even the next big community, La Ronge, that's still in the middle. Look at a map! Everybody thinks that there's the prairies and then the arctic, they always forget the bit in-between. The north is the part between the flatlands and the ice floes."

He sat back, looking embarrassed at how passionate he had become.

"Anyway, that Comfort place used to be the Marlboro. Everyone used to stay there when they came into PA, people from the fishing communities and the mines and the northern reserves. Dene and Cree and Métis and white, trappers and teachers, hunters and loggers. It was a good place. And the stories! Ai ai ai, I could tell you stories."

Just then the woman from the counter came over, giving me a cup of black coffee and him a bowl of what looked like cream swirled with fresh chocolate.

"Ekōsi," he said.

"You are always welcome, uncle. Your breakfast will be ready soon."

He nodded, then spoke to her while he looked at me.

"I was going to tell my friend here some stories from the old days," he said, "about what happened in the back streets of PA when you were young, but perhaps he's not ready for those truths just yet. Sometimes the past is still in the present."

She stepped back as if shocked, looked at me quickly then turned away.

"I'll get the food," she said.

There was a silence while he sipped his drink, making a slurp and leaving a thin white moustache on his lip.

"What is that?"

"The best cappuccino in the north," he said, "made with fresh milk and hand shaved Belgian chocolate. My niece has many talents."

"So, what was so special about the Marlboro?"

"The parties," he said, without hesitation. "The people who came to stay there, they were from the north, from dry reserves or bush camps, they were always with their small groups of family and workers. Then they came here, and they enjoyed themselves. Oh, how they enjoyed themselves! Each group would have a party room, a special room they'd booked and where they'd arranged for the booze to be delivered.

"If you flew in on Saturday night or Sunday, see, all the liquor stores and take-outs were closed. So, they'd send money down to someone like me, who lived here, and I'd get a taxi driver to deliver to the hotel. The folks would come down, get changed, and then just spend the evening going from floor to floor. I never understood why the organizers expected anyone to show up at the Monday morning conference sessions. I'd go there, because in those days I didn't drink, and the conference room would be empty except for two or three people and all these chafing dishes full of eggs, bacon, sausage. They would be happy to see me and have someone eat the food they had prepared. Oh, it was a good time."

At that point our food arrived. We each had a large croissant filled with ham, a fried egg, cheese, crème fraiche, and some sort of salsa. It looked magnificent, and it tasted delicious. We both ate in silence for while, stopping only to sip at our coffee.

"Of course, it wasn't all parties and fun," he said at one point, taking a breath about half-way through his sandwich. "There was a lot of booze, and sometimes that led to problems. I heard once that someone had got into a fight and been stabbed. He'd got as far as the elevator but had collapsed on the floor inside. People just got on and off, stepping over him, standing to the side of him, thinking he was drunk, and he went up and down the hotel for nearly an hour before someone realized he was hurt and called for help. Amazingly he didn't die, though."

We continued eating and finished our croissants, using the last piece of pastry to wipe up any left-over sauce. I ordered another coffee but he declined, saying one cappuccino was enough to last the day. It was only after mine arrived, after the waitress had cleared the plates and his niece had checked on how we'd liked the food, that he started to talk again.

"I think I have found you a canoe," he said. "It is a good canoe, strong and sturdy, and able to fit you and your bag with comfort. There are also two paddles, one to use and one to keep as a spare, and a small anchor. It can be available as a trade for the truck. But you should know something. My fee is the dog."

"Badger?" I said.

"That is a good name. He will be a strong hunter. Yes, Badger. For two reasons. One, because he is a good dog and will be good company for me, and second because I do not think he would be good in a canoe. Even his name should tell you that. A badger is a digging animal, a lover of earth and trees and muddy banks where he can scratch out gophers, voles, mice. He doesn't fish. He doesn't swim. He can, but he doesn't want to unless it is necessary."

I thought back to the coulee and remembered that Badger had never once jumped into the river with me. I nodded, reluctantly.

"If he will go with you," I said.

"Oh, there is no doubt. I knew it as soon as I saw him."

I drank some more coffee before asking the next question.

"So, how does this trade work?"

"With trust," he said. "I will take you to show you the canoe, and if it is acceptable to you then we will put the paddles into the truck. Then I will leave you and Badger with the canoe while I take the truck to show to the man who owns the canoe. Then if the truck is acceptable to him, he will come back with me. He will give you the paddles, you will give me Badger, and we shall all go away happy."

I thought it over but could not see any flaws in the plan.

"When?"

"It is a good day for trading," he said. "Leave a good tip."

He got up and walked out of the café. I went to the counter and paid, it was a reasonable bill and I left a 30 per cent tip.

"Fifteen per cent is fine," said the woman with the dark hair, grinning. "He's not my real uncle!"

I smiled back and shook my head, then followed him out on to the busy street. He cut through a couple of empty lots and a back alley, and it seemed like it only took ten minutes to return to the hotel. When we got to the truck Badger did not bark at all. He just moved over into the back seat and sat quietly while we got in.

I followed directions as they were given and in a few minutes we were back at the river, driving along with the water separated from the road by a grassy bank. There was a bench on the bank, with someone sitting on it, and I was told to pull into a nearby parking space.

"Take the key with you, but don't lock the truck," said my guide.

Once we were out of the car he pointed across the street.

"This seemed an apt place to make a trade," he said.

I looked over the road and realized we were in front of a brown brick building with a green façade running above the windows.

"That's the North West Company store," he said. "They've been trading here for 300 years, since before the Hudson's Bay Company even came to this part of the country. If you take this canoe and follow the river, you will pass a place called Cumberland House. That was where Peter Pond stayed, in 1779. He travelled from there all the way up to Lake Athabasca, trading with the Chipewyan Dene people and the Cree for beaver. When he left, he took nearly eighty thousand pelts back with him to Montreal. Eighty thousand! In one season. When the North West Company was established, they had sixteen shares, and Peter Pond had one of them. You will be travelling a famous highway, this river. Come."

We walked over the grass and down to the river, where a long green canoe was tied up to the bank. I pulled on the rope and the canoe came into the shore. Once I had its nose in the reeds, I looked at it more closely. It was aluminium, about sixteen feet long, I guessed, and the back end was square, like on a regular boat.

"That's so you could put on a motor if you wanted," he said.

There were two small seats, one at the back and one

more in the front, and a couple of thwarts, cross braces that were connected to metal rods on the floor. The vertical struts left small gaps next to the skin of the canoe.

"The paddles go along the sides there, if you have to portage."

I grunted, just to show that I was listening and also that I did have some idea of what I was doing.

I pulled the prow in as tight as I could then stepped over and sat down. It felt comfortable and I could not see any chips, cracks, or water stains which might indicate leaks and other future problems. The beam was wide and stable, and I felt very settled and secure. I climbed back on to the bank.

"It's a good canoe," I said. "This would be a fine trade."

My guide nodded, then turned and walked back up to the road. As I followed him up the embankment, I saw that the bench was now empty and as we approached, he gestured that we should sit. He offered me a cigarette, but I declined. He lit his own, and we sat and looked at the river.

"What do you think of this Alsama business?" I said.

"Me? I don't think anything. It's white man's business, nothing to do with me. Something for you moniyâw to worry about."

"But what about the Treaties and everything? What about Indigenous rights?"

"What about them? My friend, our Treaties are with the British crown, not with Canada, or with Alsama either. Who is in government here does not matter, when it's to do with Treaty Rights then we speak to the Queen.

"Anyway, our Chiefs tell us not to be concerned. The leaders of this new country, Alsama, have told the Chiefs that our languages will be protected. Not only protected but honored.

"They negotiated with us and promised that bilingualism will no longer mean English and French. Instead, everyone will have to learn Cree, or Dene, or Blackfoot, or Sioux. They promised that our history will be taught in schools, and that our schools on reserve will get the same funding as schools for white kids in the cities.

"They promised us new houses, built strongly so that each family can have its own home, and clean water in every community. For these things, we agreed to stay neutral. We promised not to resist, not to take up arms against the invaders who came to help them separate from Canada.

"So, when the foreigners came, we stayed home. We kept our promises. We are waiting, now, to see that they keep their promises as well. We learned from the last treaties. We set some deadlines, a timetable. We were promised progress within two years. We shall see."

He finished his smoke, stubbing it out with his foot, then lifted the filter and put it in his pocket.

"It's best not to leave traces," he said. "You never know who will follow your trail."

He stood up and led me to the truck. We leaned on the side and I saw that there were now two paddles in the tray, along with a bright orange life jacket. I realized that the man who I had seen sitting on the bench when we arrived must have been the person who had brought the canoe. He had had time to check out the truck while we were down by the river.

Uncle smiled as he saw comprehension dawn on my face.

"Yes, the trade is good," he said. "Give me the keys, take your stuff, and go."

I opened the door and reached in past Badger, who sniffed my hand. I scratched his ears.

"Have a good life," I said, softly, then pulled out my pack from the back seat. I handed the truck keys over, slung my pack over my shoulder, put the paddles under my arm, grabbed the life jacket, and walked away down to the river.

I heard him calling after me.

"Go across the river as soon as you can. There is a weir, not too far, and it is best to stay on the north side. And remember, others have made this journey before you," he said. "Most of them survived."

After I had loaded the canoe, I untied the rope and maneuvered it so that it was broadside on to the bank. I stepped over the gunwale and sat down on the stern seat, paddle in hand. I reached out with the blunt end and, as I pushed away from the bank and felt the current take me, I looked back up the hill. The truck had gone.

CHAPTER 13

THE BRIDGE RECEDED BEHIND me as I slowly got the feel for the canoe. It sat well on the water, and I was really just guiding it as I floated down the gentle current. I tried paddling a bit, to make it go faster, and that seemed to work fine as well. I soon got into a rhythm and found myself enjoying the journey. I remembered what Uncle had said about the weir and so I crossed to the north side, where I kept as close to the bank as I could.

The traverse of the river was fine, there wasn't much of a breeze, and the only consternation happened when I got too close to a couple of pelicans. Close up, they were a lot larger than I had imagined, and their beaks looked quite dangerous when they swung their heads around towards me, their saggy necks wobbling. I splashed the water with my paddle, and they swam away.

I soon came to the weir but found the channel that took me past it safely. Then I went past a big pulp and paper mill, the smell drifting down from the towers strong enough to make me want to retch. The river was still calm and placid, and I made good time all the way down to Cecil

Ferry, where a chain-link cable pulls a boat full of six cars at a time across the river. The ferry was on the south side as I passed, but some people waved at me from the deck, so I waved back. After the ferry the river started to meander more and the current increased. I found small rapids building up on the corners of the bends and to avoid them moved a bit further out into the middle of the river.

I must have been paddling for almost four hours when suddenly I saw a line of waves stretching right across the river. I tried to get in closer to the bank, but the current was faster here, and I kept getting splashed each time I turned across the line, water sploshing up over the side of the canoe. As I approached the rapids, I turned the canoe back to the centre again, so I was looking straight at the waves, and as I entered the turbulence, I felt the canoe being lifted and shaken. I just kept alternating sides with my paddle strokes, desperately hoping there were no rocks sticking up from the riverbed. Then the waves were gone, and the river was its normal placid self again, and I realized I must have been holding my breath for I sagged back in the canoe, exhausted. Exhausted and relieved.

I went back towards the north shore again and this time pulled into the bank to catch my breath. I held on to a couple of willow branches that arched down into the water, holding myself steady in place. A pair of red-winged blackbirds chattered at me from higher up the tree, and a small flock of geese circled round to land further down the river. It was very peaceful.

On the south side of the river was a large concrete wall, covered in graffiti, it looked like it was the remains of an old dam or power station of some sort. I pulled out my highway map but could find no mention of the rapids I had just survived, or of this relic from the industrial age.

It looked like it would be about sixty kilometres from Prince Albert to the confluence of the two rivers, but as I didn't really know how fast I was going, I had no idea when I might get there. Once I felt rested, I pushed out from the shore, and started paddling again.

It turned out that I must have been travelling at about seven kilometres an hour. The sandy hills got higher and the spruce trees more majestic, and then I realized that there was a gap to my right. The south bank had disappeared, and there were small eddies and ruffles on the surface of the river. I was at the forks, the place where the North and South Saskatchewan rivers come together, and it was late afternoon.

I had been paddling for over eight hours. I decided to find a place to camp for the night, but the shore was lined with deadfall and I couldn't figure out how I would make my way through the debris. Eventually I saw a small sandy beach, where I was able to pull in and drag my canoe up out of the river.

I cut some willow and stuck four stems into the sand, then tied a corner of the tarp to each stem to provide some shelter should it rain. My sleeping bag I simply stretched out on the sand. I made a small campfire and boiled water for coffee, ate my sandwiches, and went straight to sleep.

THE NEXT MORNING when I woke up, I could hardly move, I was so stiff and sore. I guess my hours spent in the gym had not prepared me for real world exercise. I tried to stretch as much as I could, then decided just to work out my muscles by paddling.

According to my map, it was about twice as far to my

next barrier, the Squaw Rapids Dam at the eastern end of Tobin Lake, as it had been to get from Prince Albert to the forks. Even allowing for the fact that I was referring to a road map, it was a good bet that this next stage would take me two days. I figured I would paddle until I was too tired to go any further, then find a campground for the night. And that's what I did.

The river was straight on this stretch and the paddling was easy. There were no ferries, although at one point some power cables swooped down in a parabola over the water. In the middle of the river the clearance was only a couple of metres, and even on the north passage I felt I had to duck as I went underneath. I was glad not to be paddling in the early summer, when the river would be high with meltwater from glaciers in the Rockies.

That afternoon I stopped early to make my camp. I had passed a number of old cabins, but most were either falling down or semi-submerged in the river itself, so when I saw one standing on a gravel beach that rose up from the river, I decided to stop for the night. The cabin was in reasonable shape, and the base slats of the bottom bunk seemed firm.

As I poked around, I found the remnants of a newspaper, just three or four pages. It was an old issue, two or three days out of date, and had no doubt been left by a fisherman who had also stopped overnight. I guessed that the rest of the paper had been used as a fire starter and thought that I would do the same. Before I crumpled it up, I scanned through the stories.

It was a weekly paper, the *Nipawin Journal*, and in addition to community notices and the results from the local baseball league, I found a section called "in other news". This gave a summary of what had been happening in the region, and in this new country that Uncle had described.

I found that as he had said, things were generally settling down. The three governments had obviously been planning this for some time, and Alsama appeared to be fully functional. There was still some tension with the rest of Canada, especially Ontario and Quebec, but the borders were now firmly established.

The American troops had been withdrawn to the base at Wainwright, from where they could be deployed if required, but most people were acquiescent to the new regime. The Canadian forces had been given the option of staying in Alsama or returning to Canada. Those who chose to leave had been repatriated, although they had been commanded to leave their weapons behind, while the others had formed the nucleus of a new military organization, the Alsama Defence Force, or ADF.

The Northwest Mounted Police had been brought back to life and, together with the ADF, were responsible for overall security. They had taken over most of the civilian policing duties outside of the main cities and were also seeking out saboteurs and resistors.

The paper had a story about the trial of five resistance fighters who had been captured trying to blow up the Gardiner Dam, south of Saskatoon. They had been caught on the banks of Lake Diefenbaker and given a very quick trial before being sentenced to a six-year prison term at a new jail which was being built in the Qu'Appelle Valley. Other jails were being constructed in Kananaskis Country, south of Calgary, and in the Riding Mountain Provincial Park in Manitoba, so I figured there must be more resistance than was being reported.

In more local news, it seemed that the police in Prince Albert were looking for someone who had severely beaten a sex worker, but there were no stories of mislaid canoes or an abandoned truck with Alberta number plates, so I figured I was safe. Once I had read the paper, I carefully folded each sheet, starting at one corner and ending up with a long thin swatch. This I rolled into a tight ball, starting at one end of the swatch and tucking the other end into the middle of the ball, holding the rolled paper together. I ended up with four of these fire starters and put them into the wood stove. I made a pyramid of kindling around the paper, and with one match the fire caught.

I rolled out my sleeping bag and left it open so that it could air out. The fire soon got a good draught going and the cabin warmed quickly. I had been nibbling on my dried fruit and nuts throughout the day but was feeling hungry, so I dug into my pack and found my fishing line and lures. It was as I pulled them out that I realized they were folded inside my river maps, which I had forgotten about. I quickly checked and was grateful to realize that there were no more rapids in my near future.

Putting the maps aside, I rigged up a fishing rod using a yellow five of diamonds lure and went down to the edge of the gravel beach. I tied one end of the line to a small sapling growing out of a crevice, and cast out with an underarm motion. The lure dropped with a splash and I counted to five, then trolled back in the old-fashioned way, hand pulling the line and rolling it up on the stones. Nothing happened, of course, so I kept trying, changing the number I counted so that the lure went deeper each time. At eight I suddenly felt the pull and knew that I had a fish on the lure.

I pulled in the line steadily and was delighted to see a good-sized pickerel. I lifted it from the water, held it by the belly to avoid the nasty spines on its dorsal fin, and cracked it on the back of the head with my knuckles. I threw it a bit higher up the beach, then cast out again. Soon I had three good sized fish and went back to the cabin. I cleaned the fish, then brought out my camping pan and put it on the stove to warm through. I had no oil or butter, but I figured if I turned the fish a few times it wouldn't stick too badly.

The coffee perked at the same time as the fish started to flake, and I had a wonderful supper sitting on the small white plastic chair that had been left outside the door, looking out over the river, listening to a loon calling, and admiring the sunset. I looked at my river maps and it seemed that the next day, when I hoped to cross Tobin Lake, could be a bit more problematic.

It was a large lake and known to suddenly freshen up with unexpected winds that chopped the surface and made canoeing difficult. I turned in early and slept well, woken only once in the night by the sound of something walking on the gravel near the cabin. I thought it might be a bear, drawn to the smell of cooked fish, but I just lay still, and the steps moved away.

In the morning I went down to the river to get fresh water for my coffee and saw deer tracks in the sand between the gravel and the water. That explained the steps in the night, I realized, and I breathed easier. I knew that there were bears around but hoped they would be further inland, feasting on blueberry and saskatoon bushes as they built up their fat reserves for winter. It did make me think that I needed to be better with food storage, though, and from then on, I cooked and ate some distance from my sleeping bag.

After breakfast I set off again, this time keeping to the south bank of the river as I wanted to minimize my exposure to the open water of Tobin Lake. My charts showed a maze of small channels, but the main current seemed to go in the right direction, and the winds never really picked up. It was a steady paddle, and I got my first sight of the big dam in the late afternoon.

I knew from my river map that there was a seven kilometres long portage here, and I wasn't sure when the dam workers would finish their shift, so I pulled into the bank and carried my gear, including the canoe, up to the treeline at the top of the grassy slope. There was a handmade sign nailed to a tree, with an arrow pointing up a trail into the woods, and I figured that was the trail which made the portage around the dam. I heard car engines at around five and assumed that was the shift change at the dam, if indeed anyone was left there overnight.

I didn't see any human beings all afternoon, although a large moose did emerge from the bushes and go down to the river for a drink. It was beautiful to watch, the sun gleaming on her flanks as she stood in the shallows. I didn't move but perhaps she caught my scent, for she suddenly turned and trotted off back into the woods. I sat under the trees until just after six, which I figured would give me two hours before sunset.

At that point I stood up, stretched, then tucked the two paddles into the gaps along the inside of the canoe. I looped my life preserver into the straps on the backpack and put that on, then lifted the canoe up over my head and settled it onto my shoulders. The little plaque on the stern said it weighed seventy-five pounds, which I thought was an acceptable weight. I had certainly bench-pressed much more than that at the gym. I shuffled around until it felt balanced. Then I started walking up the portage trail.

It took me nearly two hours to walk the trail, pausing for breath more and more frequently as time went on, and the sun had nearly disappeared when I came out of the trees and found myself on another grassy slope, this one leading down to the river. There was still enough ambient light to see, so I put down the canoe and set up my tarp at the edge of the trees. My shoulders ached, and I was tired, so I ate the last of my dried fruit and went straight to sleep.

I slept for ten hours, waking up just as the sun was starting to rise over the river. I felt hungry but refreshed. I badly needed a coffee, but I didn't want to stay around the dam any longer than necessary, so I loaded the canoe and slipped away as quietly as I could. It was a cool still morning, with some wisps of fog lifting off the river, and I paddled as though in a dream.

I let my fishing line spool out behind me, hoping to catch a pickerel for my breakfast. I had tied a wooden match into the line, and when it suddenly snapped, I knew I had a bite. I quickly put my paddle into the canoe and started to pull on the line as I drifted down the river. The weight was heavy, and the canoe swung sideways around as the line strained. I cursed, knowing I had caught a deadfall, a submerged log that was now acting as a sea anchor. The canoe basically stopped but the river didn't, and small waves started lapping up against the sides and into the bottom by my feet.

I was starting to get concerned when the log jerked loose and started floating behind me, I could tug it more easily. The canoe started drifting again and I managed to hold the line in one hand and lift the paddle with the other, using the oar as a rudder to turn the canoe into the current and facing downstream. Once that was accomplished, I replaced the paddle and started pulling in the line with both hands. It was a slow process as the log was heavy, but eventually the end of the line broke water alongside the canoe. I looked down and got the shock of my life. An eye was staring at me.

I managed not to drop the line. As I looked more closely, I realized that I was looking at the long, pointed head of a jackfish, or northern pike. The yellow flash of the lure hung precariously from its lower jaw, but somehow the line had become wrapped around the head and the fish was immobilized. It was also very big.

I had caught pike before, and knew they were a bony fish but with good fillets if you could get at them. I also knew they were vicious, with sharp teeth and the habit of biting anything within reach. Not for nothing is it known as the 'water wolf'. I wasn't keen on the idea of having it in the canoe with me, at least not when it was still alive, so I held it as tight against the canoe as I could, gripping the line with one hand while using the other to pick up the paddle and steer myself to shore.

The current was gentle and hugged close to the shore, which helped me come into the bank, but I had to coast along for nearly ten minutes before I found a place I could safely land. As I edged into shallow water the fish got more distressed and agitated, so I reached over and smacked it sharply on the head with the base of the paddle.

This stunned it long enough for me to clamber out of the canoe and drag the pike up onto the sandy bank. I turned around to get the knife from my pack and found the canoe had drifted away. Luckily the current was slow, and I was able to splash in and grab the stern, then drag it back to the beach. I tied a rope from the canoe to a stunted tamarack growing in the shallows and turned back to the fish only to find that it had woken up and was slithering back down the bank.

Quickly I grabbed its tail, which was wet and slimy, and pulled it back up the grass. I grabbed a nearby rock and hit it hard on the back of the head, twice, this time killing it. I was panting as I sat back next to my trophy.

The fish was huge, the length of my arm from hand to shoulder, green with yellow spots and shading to a pale white along its stomach. At its deepest it must have been eight inches from dorsal fin to belly. I had never caught a fish so big before. I took my knife and cut the line, unwrapping the filament and carefully removing the lure. My lucky five of diamonds, I thought, I shall keep this one as a memento.

I cut out the guts and stomach, finding a good-sized pickerel as proof of its earlier breakfast, and tossed the entrails into the shallow water. I rinsed the cavity in river water, then carefully filleted as much as I could of the meat. I ended up with three good sized fillets, more or less devoid of bones, and two more shredded fillets where I had practised my technique. I lit a small fire and cooked those two for breakfast. The other three I wrapped in one of the maps I had, one which focused more on the Alberta rivers, and then placed them out of the sun in the bottom of the canoe.

Breakfast finished, I cleaned up, got back in the canoe, and pushed off from the bank. I hadn't gone more than a couple of metres when a large bald eagle swooped down and landed on the bank where I had cleaned the pike. He started pecking at the remnants happily, only to be disturbed a minute later by two ravens who flew in to share the feast. I left them to it, but the cawing and croaking continued to be audible long after I had rounded the bend and was out of sight.

THAT NIGHT I found another old cabin, this one on a high bluff near where a smaller river flowed in from the north. I pulled the canoe up out of the water and turned it over, carried my pack and the wrapped pike fillets up to the cabin, and settled in for the evening. I ate outside as it was a clear quiet night, and the northern lights appeared as bands of green.

These soon turned into sheets of yellow, blue and red, shimmering across the sky. Suddenly the bands seemed to merge into a single strand, which then formed a circle, the light pulsating as though the aurora was spinning. I watched in awe, I don't know for how long, and then as suddenly as they had arrived, the lights disappeared.

I slept soundly that night, whether it was the effect of the lights or being in a warm dry space, and when I woke the sun was already high. I decided to have a day off from paddling and spent the time fishing for pickerel from the edge of the bluff. I caught a half dozen or so, which I cleaned and ate. I looked at my maps, and figured it was about three days from where I was to the big dam at Grand Rapids, just before the river entered Lake Winnipeg. I would pass close to two communities and would have to navigate the expanse of Cedar Lake, but if my luck and the weather held then I should soon be almost at the end of the river section of my journey.

And that's how it went. I slid under the bridge at Pemmican Portage in the very early hours, not disturbing even the ghost of Peter Pond as I travelled past Cumberland

House. At dawn there was suddenly a shot, it was really loud and gave me a heck of a shock.

Then a big moose came crashing out of the bush and jumped into the river, and there was another shot.

The bullet seemed to just whiz over my head, and I called out, 'don't shoot, I'm not a moose' or something equally silly. The moose veered off and I got a brief glimpse of someone with a rifle, he came out of the trees and stood on some rocks, but I was paddling pretty quickly to get away and I wasn't really sure whether it was just a trick of the light.

It must have been a weekend when I got The Pas, the river was full of rafts and kayaks and even big fat inner tubes, all full of loud giggling children or quiet teenagers surreptitiously drinking beer. Nobody took the least bit of notice of me, except for giving me a couple of waves, and I paddled through and out the other side without causing any ripples. I passed under the railway bridge and thought momentarily about hitching a ride across the tundra to Churchill, but the idea quickly passed, and I focused on finding my way into the correct channel, the one which would bring me out on the south side of Cedar Lake.

It was a big lake and I stuck to the south shore all the way around. There was a wind blowing steadily out of the southwest, not strong but enough to ruffle the white caps. I hadn't seen or heard anyone for two days, not since leaving The Pas, and I didn't want to risk getting swamped.

I caught and ate fish, drank coffee, and found either a grassy knoll or an old cabin as a place to sleep each night. It was on the fourth day after I had seen the northern lights that I came out of Cedar Lake and through the narrows into Cross Lake. I realized the rock face I was paddling towards was in fact the great grey wall of the Grand Rapids Dam, clearly visible even from ten kilometres away. I knew that the river looped around to the south of the dam but that this was not really navigable, certainly not in a canoe.

According to my map, however, there was an RV park just to the north of the dam. I tried to head in that general direction and was buffeted about as I crossed the more open water of Cross Bay. It seemed at one point that the wind had veered to out of the east, and was pushing me backwards, but I was glad to at last reach the sanctuary of the shore. I tied up the canoe in some reeds about two hundred metres from the campground. Then I went to explore.

CHAPTER 14

Once I got out of the dense brush along the edge of the river, I found that there was a path running parallel to the shore. It was late afternoon, almost dinner time, and I could hear voices coming from the various camp sites around me. After spending more than a week in the quiet of the river, the sound of people talking was both loud and raucous. I tried not to be noticed as I walked quickly into the central area of the camp, where the washrooms were located.

There, as I had hoped, I found the camp noticeboard. There was the usual visual cacophony of posted information, from offers to guide fishers to the best holes to what to do if you came across a bear. There were even a number of business cards posted, although why someone on holiday would suddenly need a kitchen renovation was beyond me.

At last, I found what I had hoped would be there: a bus timetable.

It appeared that there was a daily bus from Thompson to Winnipeg, arriving at Grand Rapids at about a quarter to two in the morning and departing some twenty minutes later. The bus stop was at the Pelican Landing Gas Station and Restaurant, which I assumed would be out on the highway.

I got back to my canoe without meeting anyone, carefully hid the canoe and paddles deeper into the brush and walked out with my backpack. This time I did meet some campers, a younger couple who looked like they were heading off into the woods for a quiet romantic interlude.

The man nodded at me as we passed, holding hands with the woman who kept her eyes looking down to the ground. I strode through the central area towards the toilets, thinking I should probably see what I looked like after so much time away from such essential facilities.

The mirror, even though grimy and smeared, showed that I really needed a good wash and a haircut. The first I could achieve and did, stripping off my shirt and washing my arms and torso thoroughly. I then filled the sink with water and dunked my head, snorting like a buffalo as I came up for air and a towel. I dried off and tried to smooth my hair into some sort of place, then dug around in my pack and found a cleaner shirt before I got dressed again. The old shirt, which even I had to admit was filthy and stank of both smoke and fish, I left in the garbage bin.

Back outside I walked through the rest of the camp and left by the main gate. The attendant was speaking to a family who were checking in, and nobody paid me any notice as I started walking down the road. In less than a kilometre I was on the highway, so I turned south and walked for another three or four kilometres until I found the gas station.

I walked in and was able to buy a ticket, one way to Winnipeg for just under fifty bucks, so I paid the fellow behind the counter and then went to check the restaurant. They closed at seven and the staff were already starting to clear away the tables, but they were willing to put together a burger and fries for me as long as I went outside to eat it. I agreed, and also ordered a slice of lemon meringue pie and a coffee.

"You can get refills on the coffee at the gas station," said the young lady who served me, and I thanked her. It was getting dark, and I had almost seven hours until the bus arrived. I got my food and walked across the forecourt of the garage to a narrow strip of grass and trees between it and the road.

Here was a picnic table, located underneath a sign informing drivers of the opportunity to get gas, use the washrooms, and spend money in the shop. There was ambient light from the windows of the restaurant, where I could see the staff continuing to tidy up. I sat on the bench and spread my feast out in front of me. I tried to do the math but gave up, deciding that this was the first meal in at least the last twenty that I had not eaten fish. And had cream in my coffee. It was delicious.

After I finished my meal, I walked around a bit, up and down the road, past the gas station and back, topping up my coffee and then using the washroom, and just generally killing time until the bus came. The waitress walked out with another fellow, they both got in to their cars and drove away. A few other people arrived around midnight, some of whom nodded at me in greeting but most who ignored me. We made for a desultory and taciturn collection.

At one forty-five the bus pulled in and, to my astonishment, three people got off. Two cars at the edge of the parking lot started their engines, their headlights suddenly bright, and after getting their bags from underneath the bus the passengers went to their rides and were driven away. The bus driver told us he would load in about seven minutes, then closed the door with a pneumatic hiss and went into the gas station.

Six minutes later he came out, coffee in hand, and opened the door to the bus. As we boarded, he took our tickets, looked at them in a cursory manner, and stamped them with a small clipper he held. He made some people leave larger bags on the ground, but I kept my backpack with me, and he just waved me through. Once we were all on, he put the larger luggage under the bus, slammed down the hatch door, then came back up and stood at the front, facing the passengers.

"Just for you folk joining us here," he said, "and as a reminder to everyone else, no open booze is allowed, not on the bus or when we stop. No smoking either, not on the bus but when we have a longer break you can get off and have one if you want. No sleeping in the aisles or on the luggage racks. If you want music, use earphones – others might want to sleep. Thank you."

He made his way into the driver's seat, closed the front door with a hiss, and we started off.

I DIDN'T WANT to fall asleep, so I spent my time studying my road map. Once I had my route planned, I stared out of the window. Some people snored softly, others read a book, some talked quietly to each other. I realized how unworkable my other ideas had been and was grateful for the small taste of comfort given by the bus.

At one point I had considered trying to canoe across Lake Winnipeg, telling myself that it was only fifty kilometres from Long Point to the eastern shore. Then I had thought about hijacking a fisherman's boat from the camp ground at Grand Rapids. I knew that they motored up from the lake to the back side of the dam and then floated back to the lake on the outflow current from the generating station, fishing for pickerel. One of those boats would have surely been sturdy enough for the crossing. Instead, I was travelling through the night down the long empty highway.

At Grand Rapids I had discovered that my ticket would be the same price wherever I stopped. I therefore bought a ticket to Winnipeg but had no intention of going there. As the bus drove past the ferro-cement statue of the World's Largest Sharp-Tailed Grouse, I got my pack ready and after we stopped, I disembarked into downtown Ashern. I was at the junction where Main Street met the highway, and it was four thirty in the morning. The bus pulled away and I started walking back up the highway, towards the gravel road that led east to Hecla Island.

I got back to the grouse, which was bathed in light straying from the Motor Inn on the other corner. It was five o'clock, and soon doors started opening. The rooms had direct access from the parking lot, and people spilled out to their trucks, shouting greetings and making comments about the cold of the pre-dawn day.

They were all wearing bright orange toques or baseball hats, and shorts or jackets of the same vibrant colour. They carried long leather or soft-cloth bags, which were laid reverently in the back seat, thermos bottles of coffee or tea, and boxes of shot gun shells. These were hunters who had licences to shoot migratory game birds, heading out to the streams and rivers, lakes and fields, where they could hope to find geese, ducks, snipe, and other birds.

Although most of the trucks had groups of three or four friends travelling together, a few had only a lone occupant. I identified one such fellow, an older gentleman who was fussing around trying to get his gear packed away, running back into his room three times for different things he had apparently forgotten. I waited until he came out the third time and then approached him.

"Would I be able to grab a rid with you to the lake?" I said.

He looked me up and down.

"Where's your gun?"

"I'm not hunting," I said. "I'm meeting my cousin. He and his wife are at the Hecla Island campground. I was supposed to go over with them yesterday, but I got busy at work and couldn't get down here until this morning's bus. So, I'd just like a ride as far as you're going."

"OK," he said. "Toss your pack in the pack, I'll be ready in a minute."

I did, and he was, and soon we were on the road, so far behind the other trucks that the gravel dust had subsided. He chattered on a bit, but then realized that I wasn't really answering, so he turned on the radio instead. I must have dozed, because I jerked awake when he stopped.

"You are alive, then," he said. "Here is the road into Hecla and the camp, I'm going straight down to Riverton so you're on your own now. It's about twenty klicks in but you should be able to get a ride."

"Thanks," I said, then got down out of the truck, I reached into the tray and got my pack, then waved as he gunned the engine, spun the tires on the gravel, and roared away. As the dust subsided so the silence descended. It was still dark, but I could see the faintest smear of colour in the eastern sky, so I knew that dawn was not far away.

I started to walk down the road towards the small causeway that crosses to the island and had not got very far when suddenly a war erupted around me. The goose hunters were obviously determined to have a high bag rate that morning. After a while the cacophony subsided, and from then on the guns fired in a more hesitant fashion, only one or two at a time.

I walked for a couple of hours and got so used to the distant bark of shotguns that it came as a surprise to realize that they had stopped. The sun was well up now, and I could hear birds signing from the bushes as I walked along. Some late migrating warblers, I assumed, or perhaps forest birds from the north come down to central Manitoba for their winter vacation.

They were pleasant company and the kilometres passed as I strode down the gravel road. In the late morning a truck came up from behind me and offered me a ride, which I accepted. He was another hunter, and three mallard ducks lay on the back seat of the truck. I asked him how the morning had gone.

"It was kinda quiet," he said. "I was in the blind by pre-dawn and ready to hunt as soon as we're allowed, which is half-hour before sunrise. But some young idiots started shooting as soon as they could see the ducks or geese through the haze, even though they were miles away. Big blazes of gunfire and not a bird down. Then we had to wait until things got calm and the next flights came in. The idiots got bored and left, so that was good, and the third or fourth flight came right in over my head and so I got me some supper. Doesn't happen everyday, though. Guess that's why they call is a sport and not shopping."

He laughed wheezily and lit another cigarette. It wasn't long before we got to the resort and I jumped out, telling him that I was meeting an old friend there. He waved at me as he drove away up to the campground, where I now knew he put his trailer every fall for the first three weeks of bird season. I walked slowly into the resort but as soon as he had gone, went back to the road and then found the path which led down to the lake.

The village runs along the lake, various restored houses and shops representing life in the early days of the Icelandic settlement here. I made my way down to the church and settled down among the shrubs at the back of the graveyard. I stayed there until dark, keeping still on the few times that a late visitor made his or her way along the self-guided trail.

Just before sunset I came out of hiding and walked back along the lake, past the memorial plaques and the icehouse to the old wharf and fish station. As I had hoped, the small dory I had seen during my first walk through the village was still there, pulled up on the gravel next to the display centre, and it was a two-second job to cut the painter and manoeuvre the little craft down to the water. There was a cracked paddle lying in the dirt and I took that with me, launching out into passage between Hecla and Black Island.

The night was cool but clear, with a decent quarter-moon, so I could keep the mass of Black Island on my left without too much trouble. Once around the southern tip I could see some lights over the water, and I spent most of the night slowly paddling my way across to the mainland. I hid the dory among some of the rocks on the shore and threw a few black spruce branches over the lot. Soon it looked like just another brush pile. Then I found a narrow cleft between two boulders and hunkered down there for the rest of the night and into the morning.

THERE WAS QUITE a bit of rain that morning and I got soaked, but it was good as it kept most people inside. My old road map was still useful here and told me I was either in Seymourville or Manigotagan, I wasn't sure which. In the early afternoon the rain got even stronger, and there was nobody in sight anywhere. I left my hiding place and wandered along the street which led up from the lake.

Wherever I was, there was not very much to look at, a scattering of vinyl sided bungalows and split levels interspersed with double-wide trailers. There were also a lot of building plots for sale, especially on the lake front side of the road, and I supposed a lot of people from Winnipeg liked the idea of a two-hour drive to a cottage by the lake. I wasn't much interested in that, though, so I just wandered quietly along checking out the cars in the driveways.

It wasn't long before I found an old Toyota Corolla, rusted at the wheel wells, with the keys in the ignition. Country ways are similar everywhere, I guess. I got in quietly and half-turned the key, delighted to see an almost full tank of gas.

I looked across the drive to the pale, yellow house. It was a bi-level design, sitting in the middle of the lot, the grass surrounding it straggly and unkempt. A child's tricycle lay on its side next to the steps. There were blinds at the windows, some open but most of them closed, and I could see the blue flickering of a television set.

It was about thirty yards from the car to the steps, and the drive was on a slight incline. I put the car in neutral and released the handbrake, then got out again and pushed as hard as I could. The car rolled backward down towards the road, crunching on the gravel in a way that sounded loud to my ears but obviously did not disturb anyone inside. Once on the road I got in, turned on the engine, and drove off as quickly as I could without spraying gravel.

I drove for just under an hour and reached Bissett,

where I saw a dozen motorbikes parked outside a long low log building. I pulled in next to a mud-streaked sedan and parked between it and the Harleys. I was able to buy a couple of sandwiches at the grocery store, plus some beer and snacks, and thought about what else I might need.

A tall fellow was in front of me at the counter, buying cigarettes, and from the back he reminded me of Josef's son, Adam. Then he turned around and nodded at me as he walked past, the matted unkempt beard and jagged scar running across his cheek showing me that I was mistaken.

After I had paid for my purchases, I asked a couple of the bikers which way they had come. They told me they'd come up from Whiteshell, in the south, and that the road was soft after the rain but generally passable. I thanked them and headed back out of the store. I decided that it would be best to have a full tank of gas, just in case, so I filled the truck and went back inside to pay. Then I left the store and drove down through the park.

It was a long slow drive, a twisting road through the trees. Now and then another vehicle passed me, coming up from the south. Once I had to slow down for a couple of deer wandering along the edge of the road. Sometimes I drove past a lake, the sun shining on the still damp rocks, every so often a pick-up truck or a battered car parked at a trailhead so the occupants could walk into a favourite fishing hole. Most of the time, though, it was just me and the trees.

I looped east onto another dirt road. At Bird Lake I pulled off into the campground there and set up my tarp. The campground was empty, and I found a good site on a ridge looking over the lake. I got a fire going, then went down and cast for an hour or so, picking up three or four decent sized perch for supper. I cooked them up, then ate as

I sat and drank my beer and watched the stars, thinking about my journey.

I slept well and woke quite refreshed. Then I left the car and started walking. It took me about an hour and a half to reach the border, where I saw the Canadian maple leaf flag hanging from a small, refurbished cottage. I knocked on the door and went in. And here I am.

CHAPTER 15

"And here you are," said the burly man sitting opposite from me across the table. He stopped taking notes and looked at me, pushing his pen through the accumulation of bits and pieces on his desk.

"A horseshoe and a thimble," he said, moving them to one side. "A red and cream striped pebble, an old napkin with a phone number of it, a bus ticket, a yellow fishing lure. All the things you talked about."

"It's like a medicine bundle," I said. "I've kept the things which are important, which are now part of my story. Sort of like aide-memoires. It will be good for my wife to see them."

"Ah, yes. Your wife. In the Soo, I think you said?"

"That's right."

"Do you have a number for her?"

"Not for her, for her parents."

He looked at me, so I recited the number, which he wrote down carefully.

"And how will you get there?" he said.

"I was hoping to drive over the logging roads until I get

to Red Lake, then take the road that runs south down towards the main highway."

"Drive in what? You walked in here."

"Ah, yes, just to see ...." I hesitated.

"I wanted to see what the situation was here, then I'd go back and bring my truck," I said.

"Right," he said.

He seemed to be thinking about something, then obviously made his decision.

"It's getting late", he said. "You can stay here tonight, and we'll figure this out in the morning."

"That's OK," I said. "I'll just get on my way and drive until dark, then sleep in the truck."

He stood up, filling the space in front of me. I hadn't realized he was so tall or wide. I also hadn't realized he had been holding a handgun under the desk, a handgun he was now pointing at me.

"It's not actually an option," he said. "You will sleep here. Come on."

He gestured the way and I preceded him into a small room. It had a tiny window up in the top corner, with what appeared to be bars across the gap. There was a narrow cot with a mattress, a blanket, and a bucket with a lid.

"It's not the Ritz," he said, "but it will be more comfortable than your truck."

Then he backed out and closed the door. I could hear the click of the lock.

"What about some food?" I said.

There was no answer. I sat down on the bed. After a while I lay down, and I must have gone to sleep.

I awakened when the door clicked open. The burly man was there again, still holding his handgun in one hand, managing a tray at the same time.

"Breakfast," he said, and put the tray on the floor. Then he backed out and the door clicked shut again. There was a large paper cup full of coffee and two blueberry muffins. The coffee was cool, and the muffins were stale, but I had breakfast anyway. Then I walked around the room a few times, sat on the bed, walked around the room again. I still had my watch, but I tried not to look at it every three minutes. The day passed very slowly. Now and again I would call out, asking what was happening, but there was never an answer.

It was early afternoon, just after two o'clock, when the door opened again. It was the burly man again, still holding his sidearm.

"There's someone coming to see you," said my guard. "Come along."

I preceded him down the corridor and back into the main office.

"Sit down," he said, so I took the same chair as before. He holstered his gun and stood by the door with his arms crossed. We didn't speak.

It was another ten minutes before I heard a vehicle drive up outside. There were heavy footsteps, and then the front door opened, and a tall man strode in. He nodded at the burly man, took off his jacket and hung it on a nail in the wall, then came and sat opposite to me. I saw the scar on his face and realized that it was the man who had been buying cigarettes at the store in Bissett.

He gazed at me steadily, then started picking up and looking at each of the items from my medicine bundle, which were still on the desk.

"You're a hard man to find, Mister, uhm, Dallas," he said, looking at my fake ID paper. "An Ian Tyson fan, are you?"

"Why am I being held here," I said. "I am a Canadian and I've come home after being trapped in the west. Why can't I just go home?"

"Well, for one thing, you're not in Canada," said the burly man. "Don't you know how borders work? First you have the exit from one country, then you have an area of what they usually call no-mans land, and then you have the entry to the next country."

He pointed out of the window. I saw trees, of course, and a small clearing, at the far side of which was another cluster of buildings.

"That's Canada, over there," he said.

"But why was the Maple Leaf flag flying outside here, then?" I said.

The two of them looked at each other.

"Ah, yes, well, that's probably my fault," said the man with the scar. "I must have hung the wrong flag by mistake. Old habits, I guess. I'm always making silly mistakes like that, forgetting things."

"Yes," said the burly man. "And pretending to be Sasquatch's cousin. Forgetting that as well."

The man with the scar laughed.

"Mea culpa," he said, and to my surprise pulled the scar off his face and the beard from his chin. He tossed them in a drawer, then looked across the desk.

"It's rude to stare, and you'll catch flies," he said. My mouth must have dropped open, for sitting in front of me was Adam, the son of Josef the farmer.

"My name is Sergeant Gavin Rashford of the Mounted

Police. My colleague is Corporal Peter Jones, who also serves as the border detachment officer here."

The burly man nodded at me.

"I've been looking for you for some time, Mister Dallas," said the Sergeant. "Although that's not your real name, is it? Is that how you see yourself? Some sort of romantic outlaw, travelling through the world on your own terms, living a life where you're the unrecognized hero? As you told my colleague here, you always like a good story, and you certainly told him one. The swashbuckling new age voyageur, walking and trucking and canoeing across the country, living on your wits and off the land, complete with a medicine bundle. That's quite the mythology you've developed."

He reached down to the side of the desk and brought up a leather satchel.

"Well, I have my own medicine bundle, with my own treasures, my own aide memoires. Let me tell you another story."

From the satchel he pulled out a plain manilla file folder, which I could see was stuffed with paper. A blue elastic band was stretched around the folder to hold the documents inside. He removed the elastic and placed the folder on the desk. When he opened it, I saw that the top page had about six lines of closely typed text, written in such a small font that I could not read it upside down. It was stapled to a few more sheets of paper and as the Sergeant fanned them out, I realized that there were six or seven separate documents. He picked up the first one but did not open it.

"First," he said, "I want to thank you for telling your story to Corporal Jones yesterday. I listened to the recording and you filled in a couple of gaps for me. That is why you had to stay inside for the morning today, as I was following up on a few things. So let me share my medicine bundle with you."

He opened the first document, scanned it, but did not read it out. Instead, he put it back on the pile, leaned back in his chair, and put his hands behind his head.

"This all started for me," he said, "when our detachment got a call about an electric bike. It had been found hidden under a pile of brush by the side of a range road, near where it crosses the highway. This was a week or so after everything started, and there was still a lot of confusion because of what happened in Calgary. Things had calmed down a bit because the western premiers had announced that they were forming a new jurisdiction, Alsama, and they had invited the Americans in to help with community control while they got the chains of command for law enforcement and the military established in the ways they wanted, going forward. The bombings and strafing in Calgary were a mistake, a rogue commander getting carried away, but once that was sorted out things got back to normal quite quickly.

"There were still communication problems, certain systems were cut off for a while, and there was some rumbling about armed resistance to what a few hotheads were calling an occupation. Most of those who complained were easterners who were working in Alsama, and who had been happily using our services while sending most of their money home. They were given a choice. If they wanted to stay and work, fine, otherwise they were taken to a holding centre that was set up at the army base at CFB Wainwright.

Because they had families down east, most of them ended up being put on trains back to Ontario and then on to the Maritimes. The same with the Canadian forces people, they were given the opportunity to stay or to leave.

"When the bike was found, there were rumours that the infrastructure would be targeted, bridges blown up and things like that. Some of the senior brass were concerned that perhaps it had been left by a saboteur. I was sent to check it out."

"Hang on," I said, interrupting him. "If you're a Mountie, how come you still have jurisdiction?"

"We reformed the original force," he said. "I'm a member of the North West Mounted Police, not the Mounties from Canada. They took our name away from us in 1920, an early example of eastern appropriation of a western resource. Our force was formed in 1873, after the Red River Rebellion. We started Fort McLeod, in Alberta, as a base from which we could control the whisky traders at what they used to call Fort Whoop-Up. We looked after Sitting Bull and his people, the Sioux, when they came north after Little Big Horn. We helped put down the North West Rebellion, we controlled access to the Yukon during the gold rush. We fought in the Boer War. We got named Royal because of that and then suddenly we were Canadian, not westerners. Anyway, no longer. We're back and it's about time, we're going to celebrate our fiftieth anniversary in a couple of years."

I laughed at him.

"Celebrate? Celebrate what? Celebrate not getting to Fort Whoop-Up until after all the whisky traders had left for the winter? Celebrate losing Duck Lake to Riel, losing Battleford to Poundmaker, losing to Big Bear at Fort Pitt? What's to celebrate there?"

"A long and storied history," he said, "and one that we intend to honour. Yes, we no doubt made mistakes. Doesn't everyone? You certainly did. And one mistake you made was that you forgot we always get our man. Oh yes, that was our motto, long before the Mounties caught up with Albert Johnson."

I must have showed something on my face, for he paused.

"That name means something to you, does it? Interesting."

He looked back at his file, then back across the table at me.

"So, anyway, I was sent out to look at this electric bike that had been found under a pile of brush. I spoke to the three young men who had found it, local lads who said that they were out driving one day and noticed it in the ditch. They didn't know how long it had been there. When I asked them if they'd seen or heard of anything else unusual, they mentioned that a neighbour of theirs, a fellow called Brian, had told them about some cattle getting out of a gated paddock. So, next I talked to Brian, who remembered being called by his neighbour to help bring the cattle home. And that led me to Dave Richmond, who told me about you.

"Mister Richmond gave me the dates that all this had happened, and that he'd left you out at his sister's place near Hanna. He called her while I was with him, and she confirmed that you were still there and didn't look like moving on too quickly. He also told me you'd come from Calgary, so I put a call in to them to see if they had any unusual reports of an electric bike or anything. I thought perhaps you'd stolen it. They got back to me a couple of days later and said there were two things I should know.

"First, the identification number on the bike showed

that it was owned by a professor at the university, one Doctor Peter Smythe. They had tried to contact him, but it seemed that he had disappeared, and his house was empty. I thought that was who I was looking for, but now that I've met you, I'm not sure. I talked to them again this morning and they are now going to get a warrant to search the premises.

"Secondly, there had been a strange incident, two retired gentlemen had lodged a report of being mugged. They said were walking home from a coffee shop one evening when 'some yahoo rode up on a silent motorbike, threatened us with a knife, and took our money.' They were veterans of the Balkan Wars and had served in Croatia, apparently, and were pretty mad that anyone would rob them so close to home. They had waited a couple of days to report it because of all the confusion that was going on, but they were absolutely certain that it was the same day as when the separation happened.

"I now had a couple of good reasons to talk to you, possible theft of a vehicle, possible robbery with a weapon, and I could track you from Calgary to Didsbury to Hanna, so I was authorized to travel out to see you. I was also tasked with finding out as much as I could about you, including who you were. When I got there, I called the number I had been given, and spoke with Ms. Richmond. She told me you were working down in the coulee, so I went over to the house.

"While I was there this old farmer drove down with a load of hay bales, so I set up the swap. I drove down and met you and got the sense that you weren't being completely open with me. I took the truck and trailer back to the house and the old farmer drove it home, then I left and went back to Red Deer with that empty soda can. Not completely empty, though. Back at the detachment I got it submitted for DNA analysis, and I was lucky because they got it processed pretty quickly. We put you in the system but there were no matches. So that didn't help.

"My unit commander told me that we should bring you in anyway, for questioning about the Calgary incident, so I went back out to Hanna the next morning. I got there to find Ms. Richmond and her friend both feeling unwell. They told me that they thought you had drugged them. They had both woken up with headaches and found that you had disappeared with their truck. Luckily, they hadn't done their dishes yet, so I was able to take the glasses back to the detachment and get the residue analyzed. That showed traces of barbiturates and sleeping pills, which had obviously been crushed up and put into the glasses. I'm guessing that's why you made the dark and stormy drinks, so that the fizz and bite of the ginger would hide the taste.

"I put out an all points bulletin to stop the truck, but I had no idea which way you were going. On my way back to Red Deer I stopped in to see Mr. Richmond and he permitted me to collect his father's prescription pill bottles from the farm. It will only be circumstantial evidence, but they are the same sort of pills which were found in the drugged drinks.

"It must have been nearly a week later that we found the truck, up near La Ronge. The fellow who was driving it was pretty upset to be pulled over. He started claiming that we were only stopping him because he was Cree, that we were a racist occupying force, and only calmed down once we explained that it wasn't him who we were after, it was the truck. He told us that he had bought it from a Sioux guy in Prince Albert, and that he had the papers to prove it, but they turned out to be forged.

"I drove over to Prince Albert and looked around. There's a sort of medicine man type fellow who lives down by the river, just him and his dog in a tent. My colleagues in PA told me to chat with him and so I went down to his camp site. He told me that he had heard rumours about a white guy who had traded a truck for a canoe. 'A man who was lost and looking for himself', he said. I said that I was looking for you as well and he just laughed.

"I looked at the maps and figured that there was only one way you could go with a canoe, and that was east. And at some point, if you went far enough, you'd get to Lake Winnipeg and the dam at Grand Rapids. I contacted the detachment at Cumberland House and they hadn't seen you, but told me that a few days earlier a moose hunter had reported nearly shooting a guy in a canoe near there. He had been out early and was surprised when a fellow started yelling after he'd had a shot at a big bull. The canoe didn't stop but kept going east, but the hunter said it was being paddled by a skinny white guy.

"I thought that if you had made it that far then you might be good for the whole journey. I drove out to Grand Rapids and asked around the campground, a young couple told me that they'd met a 'strange dude with a backpack' when they were going out for a walk after supper. The woman said, 'he looked weird to me, I didn't like him', but they didn't know where you had come from or where you were going. I suppose when we do a proper search in that area, we'll find your canoe stashed away somewhere.

"I got lucky at the gas station up on the highway, the girl who works there remembers you buying food just as they were trying to close, you insisted it wasn't closing time yet and they had to serve you. She said they had to make you agree to eat outside. She said you kept staring at the windows, it made her feel so uncomfortable that she asked one of her workmates to walk her out to her car. A couple of other people thought they had seen someone of your description, although they could not remember the exact date, and most people agreed you were waiting for the bus. So, I sent a photograph down to Winnipeg and asked the transit folk to circulate it among their drivers. The guy on the Thompson route was just checking in for his shift and phoned me straight away, he told me that you'd got off his bus at Ashern. He'd noticed you because you didn't look like a hunter, which is what most people are who go to Ashern in the fall.

"I checked my maps and figured out that you must be trying to get to Hecla and across the channel, so I drove down there. There were a couple of marked cars at the Riverton junction, I thought it might be an accident so I stopped to see if I could help. The officers told me that they had responded a call from a couple of hunters who had got to their blind for the afternoon shoot and found an old fellow lying in it, unconscious. He was awake when I got there, they were just waiting for the ambulance so that the paramedics could check him out, and he was happy to talk to me. He said he'd picked up this hitchhiker who wanted to go to Hecla, and who had punched him in the head when he'd stopped to drop him off. He didn't remember anything else, except that it had been a skinny guy who didn't talk much."

He stopped talking and looked at me.

"You didn't know that goose hunters dig out shallow trenches to hide in, did you? I think you thought you'd thrown him in a ditch, and he'd be there for a while. That was a mistake. I got details of his truck from the old guy, then went down to Hecla and it didn't take me long to find it, parked there in the lot. But I couldn't find you anywhere, and nobody reported seeing you around or anything. I also checked out the campground there, by the way. There was nobody there, no trailers where some hunter might be camped for three weeks. You got sloppy in your story telling, didn't you? You just made that part up.

"On a hunch, I drove back from Hecla to Riverton and then went down through Gimli to the bottom of the lake, and back up to Manigotagan, then across to here. It took me over three hours, but I figured you would have holed up somewhere overnight, so I hoped I was now ahead of you. I briefed the Corporal here, and he was the one who pointed out that you might recognize me if you saw me again and take off before we could get you. He had bought the false beard and plastic scar for a Hallowe'en party he's going to in a couple of weeks, so I borrowed them from him. I slept here overnight, then the next day I went driving up and down the roads between here and the lake. I stopped for some smokes at Bissett, and it was quite the surprise when I turned around and saw you standing there. I hoped you wouldn't recognize me with the disguise, so I just kept walking, and you didn't run out or anything, so I figured that worked. I parked up on an access road to a lake near the Bird Lake turn-off, just in case you were heading down to Whiteshell, then followed you until you pulled into the campground. Then I came back here, and we got ready to greet you.

"We were going to drive up and pick you up at the campground the next morning, but then that evening I got a call. I had to go down to Winnipeg to follow it up, which is why I wasn't around to meet you yesterday. You remember that DNA sample I took from you, at the farm where we met, well it seems we have a match. It took a while for the two systems to connect but about ten days ago, the Prince Albert police responded to an incident where a young sex worker had been badly beaten and then left in an alley. According to their report, she goes by the name Rosie when she is working. They were able to pull some DNA evidence from her, some blood had caught under her fingernails where she'd scratched the guy. There was no match in their records, so they decided to enter their sample into our data base. And there seems to be a match to you, Mr. Dallas, to that sample I got from you in Hanna. I got a fellow at the University to have a quick look for me and he figures there is a high degree of comparison between the exhibits."

He sat back in his chair and looked at me. The burly Corporal, I realized, had edged a few steps closer and was now just a few feet away to my right.

"I wonder whether there is a match between this number on your napkin and Rosie's phone," he said. "That will be interesting to find out. The same way it was interesting to find out what your so-called in-laws think of you. The Corporal provided me with the number you gave him during your chat yesterday, so I called the Soo. The lady who answered called you a total waste of space and refused to talk about you, but she did say a few interesting things. First, that your name was Peter. Peter Smythe, she said. Second, that you were not actually married to her daughter, you were just living with her. 'Shacking up and sponging off her, the big fat lump,' I think she said. And third, that the last time she spoke to her daughter, she had been talking about a fellow called Albert Johnson, who was doing some odd jobs around the house. 'He was a veteran,' she said, 'down on his luck and living more or less on the street, so she gave him some bits and pieces to do and was hoping he was going to be back on his feet soon.

"Her dad was a bit calmer, and a bit more concerned. He said he didn't really know you, you'd only met once when they joined you in Calgary for Christmas a couple of years ago, but it seemed his daughter was happy, so that was all he cared about. He did mention, though, that he hadn't spoken to his daughter for a few weeks, and he was worried that she had been caught up in the trouble. He hadn't been able to get hold of either of you, and had no idea what was happening. But he did know that he had no grandchildren, and his daughter was not staying at his house."

The sergeant steepled his fingers together, elbow on the desk, and then leaned forward for emphasis.

"Which made me think, are you really Claude Dallas, or are you Peter Smythe, or are you in fact Mr. Albert Johnson. That was another call I made this morning, to the Canadian Forces Liaison Office in Ottawa. They are cautious about what information they can share, of course, but they have no record of an Albert Johnson serving in the Canadian Forces at any point in the past ten years. So, I wonder if that is your real name, or just another layer?

"It seems strange that your name for yourself would be the same as that of the Mad Trapper of Rat River, but perhaps you just keep reinventing yourself. Still, whatever your name is, it looks like I will soon have enough to arrest you and charge you with assault using a weapon in Calgary, causing mischief and disturbing livestock in Didsbury, administering a noxious substance and truck theft in Hanna, sexual assault and causing bodily harm in Prince Albert, plus assault and vehicle theft in Hecla. But right now, I have this."

He picked up a pen and fiddled around on the desk, moving my souvenirs from side to side and eventually pushing a small piece of chipped stone to the front of the pile.

"This looks to me like an arrowhead, something you picked up when you were at the ranch. Under Section Twenty of the Historical Resources Act, it is illegal to transport artefacts across the Alberta border without a letter of permission from the Minister. I don't see any such letter here, so unless you can produce one, that's the charge I will use to hold you.

"And if you're really Professor Smythe, we still haven't found your partner, have we? I got an address from her parents and the Calgary police are going to have a look around your house today. There won't be any gruesome discoveries in the freezer, will there?"

I just sat there, and took a few deep breaths, trying to calm myself. Then I made my decision.

CHAPTER 16

"In your own words, Corporal, what happened next?"

The Inspector waited patiently while the officer in front of him shuffled from side to side.

"Sergeant Rashford told the suspect that he was going to charge him and listed out the offences. The guy just sat there. Then suddenly, it all happened so quick, suddenly he just sort of uncoiled. He came up and over the desk and headbutted the sergeant, then before I could move, he had punched me in the head as well. The sergeant and I both went down and when I looked up the guy was standing next to me. He kicked me a couple of times in my ribs, took my sidearm from my holster, and then pointed it at the sergeant, who was unconscious on the floor, blood coming out of his nose and mouth. He was about to take the shot, I could see his finger on the trigger, then he stopped. He looked out of the window, and then he looked down at me and said, 'Too much noise from a gunshot, it's your lucky day.' Then he leaned over and hit me with the gun barrel, and I blacked out.

"When I came around the Sergeant was still laying

there but at least he was conscious. I turned him on his side in case he swallowed blood, and to help him breathe, and then I called in the situation. It took an hour for the response team to get here, they came up by helicopter from Winnipeg, and after we both got treated by the medics, they came out looking with us. But we couldn't see any track, we have no idea where the guy went. We had just got back here when you arrived. I think he must be in Ontario and long gone by now."

The Inspector looked across the small office to where a chair had been pushed up against the wall. Sergeant Rashford was sitting on the chair, leaning forward with his hands twisting between his knees. A motley collection of different sized band aids covered the bridge of his nose, making him look like he had been administered to by a manic four-year old. He met the Inspector's gaze.

"Perhaps," said the Inspector, replying to Jones but looking at Rashford. "So, Sergeant, let us recap as to what we actually know. You had a fellow here, who you have been tracking across the country, who might be called Claude Dallas or might be Peter Smythe or might be Albert Johnson or might be someone else entirely. You were going to charge him with the illegal transport of an Aboriginal artefact across provincial borders but never actually read him that charge. You have a DNA sample, albeit one obtained without a warrant, but no fingerprint or other identification. How am I doing so far?"

"Yes sir," said the Sergeant.

"Did either of you take a photograph of him?"

"Yes sir, I did," said Corporal Jones. "Unfortunately, it appears that he stole my phone when he escaped."

"So that's a no, then," said the Inspector.

Just then there was a knock at the door and a uniformed officer stepped inside.

"There is no truck at Bird Lake, sir, and no other vehicles either," he said. The Inspector nodded and, after the officer left, turned back to Jones and Rashford.

"Did either of you ask him what he taught at the university?" he said.

Rashford and Jones looked at each other.

"No sir," they said, in unison.

"Something else to look into, then," said the Inspector. "He seemed to know quite a bit of western history, so that might be a clue.

"The name thing is not the only anomaly," he said. "In his story he said that he'd worked in the Caribbean, but then later he claimed to have never heard of a Dark and Stormy. How is that possible? It's like a double double down there, even if you don't drink it, you know what it is. Then, if his potential mother-in-law calls him a big fat lump, how does that match with the guy who came over the desk and took you both out? I think we need to ask Calgary to prioritize a search of the address the parents gave us, and we need to get the university to see if any of their professors are missing."

"He might not be a prof," said Corporal Jones, "he could be the odd-job man who was helping them, the ex-military guy. He seemed to know a lot about army tactics and stuff, and he is obviously a bit of a survivalist, living off the land and all that. Maybe he's suffering from PTSD or something?"

The Inspector paced around the office.

"That actually might be the most sensible thing you've said since I got here," he said

"We know that the situation in Calgary wasn't nearly as bad as he described to Dave Richmond, but it could be that he saw the helicopters and the gunfire and had a traumatic episode. So, we'll circulate his description around the military support groups there as well."

"For example, if he was really a war veteran, I wonder if he is using the name Albert Johnson on purpose. Not too many people know the details of the Mad Trapper of Rat River. Do you?"

"I know a bit, sir," said Rashford. "Didn't he shoot a Mountie and they tracked him for six weeks, in the middle of winter, then got him in a shoot-out."

"More or less, yes," said the Inspector. "But what people don't know is that we still have no idea who he was. He called himself Albert Johnson to a couple of Dene guys who met him up on their trapline, but he had no identification on him when he was captured, well, killed, and his fingerprints were not on file anywhere in Canada or the United States."

"When was this?" said Jones.

"Back in the early 1930s," said the Inspector. "They had to bring in a bush pilot to help track him down. He had killed one Mountie and wounded two others. But if our guy sees himself as a hero, why use the name of a cop killer?"

The two men remained silent.

"And of course, he also called himself Claude Dallas, perhaps after the fugitive outlaw in the Ian Tyson song. He was a real person as well, killed two game wardens I believe. That was in the early eighties. He served his time and is still alive, but he must be well over seventy by now, so I don't think he is really your man. But I wonder, why was he up on Nose Hill in the first place, and why did he talk about the coyote den? So that's something else to check."

Rashford looked up.

"I don't care," he said. "I don't care if he's a professor or a veteran or a survivalist or just a guy who's left his partner.

I want this guy. He played me for a fool, and he got the better of me. Not only that but he's arrogant, he thinks he won. Giving us that story, making himself out to be a hero. All the harm he's caused, all the way across the country. I want him, I want him in jail."

"But he's disappeared, Sergeant," said the Inspector. "How are you going to find him again? He's gone. The northern boreal forest is huge, he could be anywhere."

"Yes sir. With respect sir, we have his DNA. We know what he looks like. We can work with a sketch artist and put a good picture together. If you can get permission from Canada to let me loose over there, then I can track him. He left here with no vehicle, with no supplies. It looks like he grabbed his backpack and all the stuff we had spread out on the desk. Plus, he took the Corporal's phone and gun, and my jacket, but that's all. He's going to have to steal things, he's going to have to leave traces. He did that last time, but nobody was looking so he got away with it. This time I'll be looking for them."

"He might not be over there. And he might have a vehicle. The truck he said he left at Bird Lake is no longer there. He might have played us and doubled back into Alsama," said the Inspector, frowning. He noticed the Corporal shuffling on the spot.

"Yes, Corporal?"

"Sir, I have worked with the Canadian Border Post people. They have been putting in a good surveillance system. They might at least tell us if any of their sensors got tripped earlier this afternoon. Then we'd know whether he went there or not."

"Thank you, Corporal," said the Inspector. "You and I shall walk over there in a minute and ask the question. And if the answer is yes, Sergeant, then I will ask Winnipeg for permission to proceed with your plan. But for now, you stay here, do you understand. You will not go into Canada until we have official approval for you to do so. Is that clear?"

"Yes, sir," said the Sergeant.

"Come along, Corporal," said the Inspector, and led the way out of the door and along the clearly marked path that led to the Canada border post. The Sergeant sat and waited for them to return. He knew that he would wait to see if permission was granted, as it would be easier if he was official. But whatever happened, he was going to be going after Albert Johnson or Claude Dallas or whatever he was calling himself now. That was a promise. Everyone left traces of their passing, you just had to know where to look.

Lightning Source UK Ltd.
Milton Keynes UK
UKHW010901021221
394973UK00003B/124